JUDAS PAYNE

Judas Payne was the devil's spawn, a product of rape, a half-white, half-Indian outcast who was loved only by his pretty half-sister, Evangeline. When the Reverend Payne finds the two naked in the barn, he takes out one of Judas's eyes, and Judas chops off one of the Reverend's arms and then runs for his life. He meets up with a number of colorful characters out there in the weird wild west, from a white slave-trading ex-Confederate colonel to a gun-slinging assassin who quotes scripture as he slaughters his targets. Meanwhile, unknown to Judas, Evangeline Payne has been sold to a brothel and forced to engage in the most vile sexual acts with any man who pays for it....

In the vein of Joe R. Lansdale's weird westerns, this dark novel is Clint Eastwood's Man with No Name meets *Deadwood* meets *Cowboys and Aliens*. Jump on your horse and take a ride....

Borgo Press Books by MICHAEL HEMMINGSON

The Rose of Heaven
In the Background Is a Walled City
How to Have an Affair and Other Instructions
The Dirty Realism Duo: Charles Bukowski and Raymond Carver
Auto/Ethnographies: Sex, Death, and Independent Filmmaking
Sexy Strumpets and Troublesome Trollops
The Stripper
The Yacht People
Star Trek: A Post-Structural Critique
Judas Payne: A Weird Western
The Chronotope
Poison from a Dead Sun
Zona Norte

JUDAS PAYNE

A WEIRD WESTERN

MICHAEL

HEMMINGSON

THE BORGO PRESS

MMXI

JUDAS PAYNE

DEDICATION

For Jordan Faris,

A Story from Another Life Ago

CONTENTS

CHAPTER ONE

1.

When the Reverend Jedediah Payne moved himself, his young wife, and one-year-old daughter from the comfort of city life in Boston to the hedonistic West, he had aspirations of a church, *his* church; a congregation, *his* congregation—*his* people hinged on every word he had to give on The Word. Fundamental Baptist by training, Jedediah Payne had met with opposition from his peers concerning his "unorthodox" method of rearing a flock. Unorthodox, indeed! Obviously these fools were blinded by Satan's crafty hand, as were so many in this day of advanced technologies and incessant bloodshed. It was Payne's objective to make *the people* see what was happening, just how THE DEVIL was interfering with their lives, and how they could prevent it…with *his* help, naturally. It was so simple a solution it pained the Reverend's pious heart. And if fellow "men of God" were to criticize and ostracize him, to have him expelled from the church he preached at, then he would leave this dirty, sin-infested city and go out to the new lands of America, where people who were fresh and not yet tainted would hear what he had to say—and *believe*…and follow:

Him.

Payne was thirty-seven at the time. His wife, who had just turned eighteen, was not happy about leaving Boston and civilization; however, she had married a man whose mission was to save souls, thus she was avowed to accompany him, for better or worse. Katherine Payne had married the Reverend when she was sixteen. It was a marriage arranged by her father. She was, needless to say, appalled upon learning whom her betrothed was. Katherine was a quiet, shy girl who kept to her room and the libraries, ingesting the contents of books when she could and when the time permitted. She never found boys or men appealing, the majority of them lacking in intellect or address that could cause her heart to melt (the way she believed it would when love found her in its sights). Oh, she'd had her share of suitors, all of whom she had turned away like she would a glass of sour milk. Indeed, she knew she was an attractive young woman, by their standards; but she had to wonder if some of the suitors were only interested in the dowry—her father being a rather well-to-do man of Boston society. (Her mother, alas, had been dead since she was ten, a victim of pneumonia.)

Marry a man of the cloth? And this gentleman being nearly *twenty years* her senior? She entertained thoughts of fleeing home and hiding. She could never leave her father, however...he was sick and bed-ridden.

"I *cannot* marry that man," she told her father, sitting next to his bed, her head hung low and her hands twitching in her lap like the worried and nervous girl she was.

"You will *do* as I say, *Katherine,"* he informed her. His voice was weak; he was pale and gaunt and it pained her to look at him.

"I don't love him," she said, "I don't even *know* him."

"He is a good man. He is a man of The Lord. Could there ever be a more trustworthy husband?"

"Be that as it may," she said, "I will have a life of misery. This is *1850,* Father, and arranged marriages are not the staple of a civilized soci—"

"Civilized?!" her father choked. "No, my dear, this is a *very bad* world, one that I fear may not last long; you need a good man to protect you, because I no longer can."

Softly, very softly, "I am but sixteen..."

"Old enough," was her father's reply, and *that* was that.

She could have refused him; she could have taken a stand; however, that, she feared, would have broken her father's feeble heart—not because he had any concern for Payne's interest, but the marriage put him at ease, in regards his daughter's future days and general welfare.

Before the marriage, she and Jedediah Payne had taken a number of strolls and talked. He was an astute, tall gentleman, and a good listener from what she could tell; a little too thin for her tastes, but serious and solemn, if not perhaps a bit too quirky regarding his religious viewpoints. She liked him well enough. Any man who claimed to have been visited by an angel, and talked to the angel, piqued her curiosity.

Two days after the inconspicuous, small wedding, her father passed away.

She couldn't stop crying for her father, long after he was buried. The man she called husband did not move to comfort her, did not put his arms around her like the men did in books of romance and adventure. He simply said, "The Lord called him; it was his time."

She soon learned that the only emotions Jedediah Payne felt with any depth of fervor were antipathy and anger towards those who did not agree with him, those who questioned him. He believed his opinions and positions to be virtuous and correct without debate, as if handed down personally by the Almighty Himself (and, in fact, some of what he said he claimed to be straight from the angel he met, an angel sent from God); anyone who dared question the Reverend was either "on the side of Satan" or "holding an iniquitous grudge." Paranoid, that was probably a good word for her husband, if not painfully stubborn to take a moment and consider opposing sides, and determine whether or not they had merit. Katherine Payne was grateful he was not a lawyer, like her father—her father who had become a judge and presided over the fates of many men's lives.

Their marriage wasn't consummated until three weeks after the wedding. The night of their marriage, she sat in her room under the bed sheets, quivering in terrible disquietude over what she was going to have to do. Would he walk in naked, prepared to ravish her? No. He came in clothed, all in black as was his preference, and sat on the edge of the bed, unable to look her in the eye.

"How are you, wife?" he asked.

She admitted to some apprehension; she didn't want him to know how much. She didn't want him to know that her deepest wish and desire was to run away from this room, this house, this life, and never look back.

"Do you feel unready for this part of our union?"

She nodded.

"Then it can wait," Payne said, and left her.

He wasn't being chivalrous; she knew that—he was as uninterested about copulation as she was frightened.

In regards to sexual relations in general, Reverend Payne had no opinion. Unlike other preachers, he did not fill his sermons with precautionary ambulation on fornication and the sins of the flesh. Payne was not concerned with drives that did not hinder him, as was the case of the hypocrites who did speak of it at length, almost as an obsession (and his knowledge of their frequency of brothels as "missionary work"). Payne could not understand what made men and women act so nonsensical over the matter; he failed to see the use, other than for procreation, that the act beheld. His sermons, rather, were warnings of Babylonian governments, war, and how to spot those agents of Satan who walked among us in every day life.

Finally, Payne came to Katherine's room to do his duty, because he *knew* it was his duty: the Bible instructed him so. Katherine wasn't frightened anymore—she had three weeks to prepare and ponder. By now, she was curious more than anything else. She wanted to get it over with.

In the darkness, her husband made his attempt to mount her. He was motionless for a while, did not seem to know what to do. His cold hands felt around down there, and placed himself inside her. She cried out, out to God, closing her eyes. It was over quickly. She felt a warm stickiness in and on her privates. She tried to kiss Jedediah—he *had* taken her virginity, after all, and this meant something. Payne stood, asked if she was all right. She told him yes. He apologized and left her alone.

She thought she might cry. This was horrible. But, like her husband, she ultimately had no emotional response to the matter.

This hasty act produced a pregnancy, which the Reverend seemed pleased about. Katherine was not sure how she felt; after the weeks of sickness inclined, and her belly grew, she knew the child in her would be loved by her, loved for all eternity, loved by a family. Not the most perfect family, but a family nonetheless. It was a terrible world, the Civil War was proof of this, and Katherine Payne came to realize that the finest quality of human nature was the nature of family.

Evangeline Payne was born into this world with difficulty. It was a long and arduous labor, which Katherine felt certain she would die from. She knew about the many women who did expire during childbirth; she forebode that she might follow in their path. She was bedridden for several weeks after. The doctor told the Paynes that if a large family was wanted, it would not be a good idea. Katherine was small in the hips, and maybe too young; and while she may be able to have one or two more children, any beyond that would "likely be the death of her," the Doctor confided to the Reverend, which Katherine heard outside her door.

That was fine by Katherine Payne née Blairwood. Holding her pink, soft, gurgling daughter to her breast for suck, she felt one child would be *perfectly fine*. She didn't want to go through the ordeal of labor again, *ever*. The only thing that worried her was her husband; men, she knew good and well, coveted sons (as her own father probably wished for during his waning years) to carry on the name, the heritage, the fantasy of dynasty. Was her husband that kind of man? How could she know, when she and Jedediah seldom discussed anything, or spent intellectual time together?

Reverend Payne was not certain how he felt about his daughter's birth into the world of evil, war, and men who cavorted with THE DEVIL. He was, secretly, pleased that he could produce such life from his loins, as God had created all men to do; and he was pleased with the fact that he had a young mind that he could steer in the proper direction regarding the ways of the Lord. He had hoped for neither son nor daughter, had never given it much consideration. He was not unfailing if he desired more offspring. Eventually, he supposed, he would need a son—a son he could guide into his own vocation (as his father had), a son he could look on with pride. One day he would approach Katherine about it, but not now. Payne had other things to contend with at the moment, one of which was the opposition from the rectors of his faith against his sermonizing and preaching.

He'd always been called overzealous, this was nothing new; this critical position had surrounded him since he first knew his calling, at the tender age of ten. But when he began to cast out demons and heal the meek from the pulpit, fellow preachers at his church and other Baptist establishments in the city began to let him know that what he was doing...*was uncouth.* Payne knew they envied his ability to cast out Satan's fiends from the bodies of the afflicted; those he saved were happier and bright, their eyes glimmering, singing praises to the Lamb Jesus, and Payne and *only Payne* witnessed the ephemeral ghouls scuttle away and return—injured by God—to the dark corners of their realm. As for those who did not fully heal, it was their fault and not his; their faith was weak—if it were as solid as his, their club-feet would return to normal, their blinding eyes would see, and their deafening ears would hear...

He became convinced that THE DEVIL was out to get him. Payne was leading men and women away from the Dark Prince's reign. Obviously, THE DEVIL had gotten to others in the ministry, or had planted demons in the form of men who dared quote scripture and tend to the flock. This caused Payne to be more out-spoken when addressing the church-goers.

Then he was told, by the elders, that his services at the church were no longer needed. *Satan!* Very well—he would find another tabernacle.

No others, however, wanted him.

Coming home one night, terrified by Satan's powers and his own dogma waning, Reverend Payne went to find solace in his wife. It was the first time he had ever considered talking to her. But he was alone now, so very alone, and perhaps God had forsaken him, perhaps he had done something to make God angry. He had a wife, though, so he was not that alone. He went to her room. The baby was asleep. His wife was in her nightgown, combing her hair at the vanity. She moved to cover herself. A modest young woman, he admired that.

Something queer took him over. Gazing on Katherine's white flesh, he felt a heat inside he had never felt before—other than when he was at his best form in the church—and a twitching in the loins. He was dizzy with this sensation. *I succumb to my own Darkness*, he thought—

He grabbed Katherine, throwing her on the bed. She started to protest, then looked away. She asked to have the lights turned off, but Payne was enraptured with this new sense of being and did not hear her request. He quickly took his wife, found that his erection had not diminished, and knew her again. She let out several loud sighs and groans. Good Lord, was the woman enjoying this? *He* certainly was.

2.

Katherine was not enjoying it. It was painful—not as much the first time, but still so. Her husband was being rough. Her sighs were not for joy but to let the air out, due to his weight on her frail body. She had hoped it would be as quick as that first time, but when he was done, he did it again. The sheets under her were damp with sweat and his seed. Payne said nothing to her. He stood and left her room.

3.

As quickly as the carnality possessed him, it vanished. Reverend Payne felt base, hexed. When he removed himself from her room, he went to his study, flogged himself on the back with a small whip he kept in his desk. The throbbing of his flesh made him think clear. *Very clear.*

If the infidels would not have him in Boston, he would go to another city.

He would go far away.

He would go West.

4.

Katherine Payne did not know what had overcome her husband that night, nor did she question it; and, after a few days, she did not care. She only hoped it wouldn't happen again. If he wished to lay with her, she wanted to know in advance so she could relax her mind and body and prepare to do her wifely duty. She wanted to tell the Reverend this, but she did not have the gumption. That was not a wife's place to say such things, and she did not want to incur a tirade on "submissive obligation" from him. Additionally, she was also worried whether or not the coupling would produce a second child. In her deepest fears, she saw herself having twins, since her husband had spilled his seed into her twice. She did not know how twins came about, but she thought that might be one way.

By the time they had moved out to Tyburn, Kansas, Katherine was certain that no child was going to come. She was not feeling the sickness, nor was she becoming bloated or hungry for odd foods.

She muttered a silent prayer for this relief.

5.

The minister in Tyburn, Kansas had recently committed suicide and the townspeople were in need of a new man to bring the good word. They readily accepted Reverend Payne, despite the curious rumors they heard from Boston. Payne had purchased one hundred acres of land just outside the city limits, and any man of God who could afford such a parcel was all right by the good people of Tyburn.

The land was purchased from money left by Katherine's father. Reverend Payne secured the sale with the landowner while in Boston, appalled at the price of one thousand dollars—even more appalled when he learned there was ten thousand *more* dollars in the bank that Katherine's father had left. But money was not a matter the Reverend wished to maintain or acquire. The money would be a good security, transferred from the trust in Boston to the local bank in Tyburn; and perhaps a nest egg for his heir, or heirs, should that day come.

Katherine Payne did not like the spacious land their home was on, or the animals that her husband quickly purchased. Chickens and horses and cows, and then a pig! She was a woman of the city, thrust onto this make-shift farm. She loathed the rooster that crowed in the morning—never at dawn but long after, and far into noon as well. Her husband seemed to enjoy this new life, spending time outdoors when he was not at the church, his skin going from white to red to tan. She didn't think she would adjust to this (the library in Tyburn was very small and most of the books she had already read, so she had to make special orders through the slow U.S. Mails). This was her lot, this is what she had chosen for a life (even if her father had chosen it for her). She conceded, however, that small town life might be good for Evangeline to grow up in, rather than a crowded, bustling city.

Evangeline was growing fast, now in her first year. She was crawling about, feeding from a bottle, and curious about the world around her. The blonde hair on her head was already curly and golden. Katherine knew her child would grow up to be a beautiful woman. *But you will marry whom you choose to marry*, Katherine silently vowed, *someone you truly love and care for....*

Katherine could not say she loved her husband, nor did the Reverend ever express such a feeling toward her. She had respect for him, in a peculiar way. She prepared his meals since she did not have servants as she had in Boston; she cared for him; but he would never love him, this she knew.

On the third month of their life on the outskirts of Tyburn, Kansas, Katherine Payne went out to the barn and saw a mysterious gentleman....

6.

The reader should be aware that he was not actually a man but THE DEVIL himself. Oh yes, it just so happened that THE DEVIL was weary and agitated with Jedediah Payne—the Reverend had been saying bad things about THE DEVIL for many years and while THE DEVIL had pretty much ignored it, it was time for THE DEVIL to pay the Reverend back. "What bad thing shall I do to that self-righteous, pious man?" mused THE DEVIL to his minions. THE DEVIL had tried to reach Payne in his dreams, but even there this man of God was able to fight back....

"Rape his wife!" said the minions.

"Good idea," said THE DEVIL, and snapped his fingers.

"Make her pregnant!" cried the minions with glee.

"An even better idea," said THE DEVIL, and whistled a merry little tune.

Now, THE DEVIL, as the old stories always tell, can take human form. So this is exactly what THE DEVIL did—he became a man, wandered onto Payne's land like he owned it and made his jovial way inside the barn. He would feign being wounded because women always had a soft spot for the injured. He took the form of an Indian because he knew Katherine Payne felt horrible for what the United States military had been doing to the Indians all these years.

7.

Katherine Payne went into the barn later that day. She let out a small cry, seeing the soiled, wounded Indian on the ground. The Indian appeared as terrified as she. She stepped back, touching her chest: heart pounding. The Reverend was in town, she was all alone here, and there were no guns in the house. She had heard a great deal of stories about these savages. He merely stared at her with solemn, darkened eyes. She saw that he was bleeding from the side; there was a lot of dried, coagulated blood, it looked like he'd been shot. The Indian did not get up; he lay back down, watching her. He appeared sad. Katherine felt somewhat at ease, which struck her as odd. "How did you get here?" she asked. The Indian did not respond. "You probably do not understand me," she said. "How did you come to be injured?" The Indian merely gazed at her, then closed his eyes. She feared he'd died, but he opened his eyes again. There was a glow about him, a light that made him innocent to her. He was anything but threatening. He needed help. Katherine Payne could not turn him away. "I shall return," she said.

8.

THE DEVIL smiled to himself because things were working as planned.

The woman returned as promised, with water and cloth. He tried to move away from her as she slowly approached, then decided it did not matter. He didn't have to play the wounded creature too much, she was his. She bent down, putting the cloth in water, then proceeded to clean his wounds. He was intrigued by this woman; why did such a lovely piece of female flesh marry Reverend Payne? She smelled—like a warm day in the sun, and pretty like flowers. He marveled at the smoothness of her skin, how pink it was, and her golden hair. THE DEVIL loathed all these things.

9.

Katherine was gratified the Indian wasn't being difficult, and allowed her to clean his wounds and wrap bandages around him. The white bandage soon spotted with red. She did not know how to remove bullets, if it was a bullet wound this poor man was suffering from. And what was she going to tell Jedediah when he came home? She helped the Indian up, led him to the hay by the horses, and told him to lie there. He did as instructed, watching her carefully. What had this unfortunate soul gone through? Savage or not, he was one of God's creations who needed help—and certainly her husband, *a man of God*, would agree.

She returned to the house, checking on Evangeline. Her daughter was asleep. Was she being foolish? That Indian could come in here, kill both her and the child. No—now *that thinking* was foolish. She knew not *all* Indians were maniac killers, no matter what the papers and the penny dreadfuls said; many of those people were peaceful. This Indian seemed like the latter.

She took some food out to him: dried meats and fruits. The Indian acted as if he didn't know whether to take it or not. Finally, his hand went out to the food, and he began to eat ravenously. Katherine smiled.

She was doing the right thing—*a good thing*.

She let him be, checking an hour later to see if he had gone. He was asleep.

She didn't know how she would tell Jedediah of her find, so she didn't. It was dark by the time the Reverend returned home; he had walked to town (a two hour walk, no less!), so there was no need for him to go into the barn. She would tell him tomorrow, if the Indian were still there. She hoped—and felt guilty for it—that he would go away and the whole matter would be her secret.

Katherine could not sleep that night. She was both concerned for the Indian and apprehensive of the idea that he might come in and...*no, no, Katherine, stop that line of thinking right now!*

She got up, quietly moved through the house, getting some more food from the kitchen and going out to the barn with an oil lamp. He was still in there, awake, standing, and naked. She pulled in a breath. His penis...it was so enormous. She had never actually seen her husband's, but she knew this Indian was three if not four times the size of the Reverend's... and the phallus was glowing red.

The Indian smiled at her. His teeth were a bright white, and there was fire in his eyes....

10.

THE DEVIL did not expect Katherine at this hour of night, standing before him in her night clothing, with an oil lamp and food. Perhaps she came for this, he wouldn't have to force her after all. Indeed, why would she be so clean, so sweet to smell, so pure of skin, if not for him? He grabbed her hard, pulling her close. The lamp fell to the ground, and so did the food. She tried to cry out and he clamped his hand on her mouth. He whispered, "Hush, my dear." He dragged her toward the hay-loft. She put up a struggle, but not a good one; no, she gave in too easily, too quickly. "You have been waiting for this all your life," said THE DEVIL into her ear; "since you were a little girl, I have known your true being, and the same fate shall fall upon your daughter." So he got on top of her, pried her legs open. He stroked his giant red penis. Her teeth sank into his palm as he entered her, but he did not bleed. Her eyes gazed up, bright and blue, then closed tightly. He could see it in her face: she was in pain, but there was also ecstasy; it wasn't easy to get into her but once he did her vagina became wet and clasped around him; he quickly spent himself into her, and lay on her, gazing on her skin and hair and beauty.

"This is my dark gift to you," said THE DEVIL, "and a nice slap in the face to Jedediah."

"You speak..."

"What? Like a white man?"

THE DEVIL laughed, stood up, and revealed his true form—with a snap of the finger.

"Behold, my dear!"

Katherine was not frightened; she was not surprised or horrified. She sighed, closed her eyes, said, "I should have known."

When she opened her eyes, THE DEVIL was gone.

11.

The walk from the barn back into the house felt, to Katherine Payne, like forever. She cringed, feeling THE DEVIL's seed coming out of her, running down her leg. Violated. She had just been *raped*. Couldn't Jedediah hear that? No. The sounds were not loud, and the house was placed a good two hundred feet from the barn. It goes without saying she felt quite soiled. She could smell THE DEVIL's grime and sweat on her. She wanted a bath, needed one more than anything she ever needed in her life. But Jedediah might wake up and want to know why she was bathing at this odd hour.

So she went to her bed, prayed to the Lord. Asked Him to erase the incident from her mind, if not history. How could she tell her husband? She *could* not. In the morning, she decided she *would* not.

12.

Katherine Payne's belly was growing; the sickness she'd had when pregnant with Evangeline was also present. She knew what she had to do. She attempted, on several occasions, to coax her husband into the marriage bed. He ignored her, he had no interest in the act. He said, "Woman, what has gotten into you? Only whores ask for it!"

She looked at Evangeline one night and cried, saying to her child, "You should have been a boy, this is a world of men; for a woman, there is only anguish and affliction...."

One night, her daughter put to bed, Katherine went to her husband, who sat by candlelight in the front of the house reading from The Book. She saw that he was reading from The Book of Samuel.

"Jedediah," she said, "have you noticed something different about me?"

He looked up. "What say you?"

"Look at me," she said, turning to her side, "can't you see?"

"See what?"

She sighed, then lifted up her blouse and showed him her naked belly.

"*Katherine!*" he bellowed, rising to his feet. She pulled her blouse down. "You are with child?!?" he shouted, rather stupefied.

"Yes," she answered, oh so timid and soft...

13.

Yes, Jedediah Payne was, needless to say, quite the flabbergasted man in God's flock. The last time he had relations with his young wife was in Boston. Not once since their months out here had he gone to her...touched her...or even considered the vile desires of wanton flesh.

"I cannot be the father," he realized, saying this accusingly to his emotionally embattled spouse.

"No," she admitted.

Payne was surprised by how calm he reacted; it was almost as if he was relieved that he had not spawned another offspring.

He said, flatly, "You have some explaining to do, wife."

She began to talk, fast, fearful he might stop her before she could tell her story. She told him of a wounded Indian who had been in the barn, and how she had helped clean his injuries, and how she gave him some food, and how she hoped he just might go away, and when she went to check to see if he was there, he violated her. It was against her will, she assured him of this.

There was nothing she could have done. He was a strong, irreligious animal.

She did not confess who the Indian really was. She was certain she had a hallucination, that vision of evil.

"Why..." and he cleared his throat. "Why did you not tell me of this when it occurred?"

"What would you have thought of me?" she asked.

The anger started to boil inside him. "So you only tell me when you are with child!?!"

"I did not know I—" and she began to cry.

"Look at me," he said.

She sobbed.

"Look at me, wife!"

She turned to face him.

Was she telling the truth? There seemed to be no deception. He struck her across the face, *very hard*. Katherine fell to the porch, spitting blood from her mouth. Payne wanted to kick her, boot her in the belly and flush this evil tot from her bowels. He stopped, taking heed of what he had done. She lay at his feet, choking.

He couldn't do it. It would be murder. He wouldn't do it.

"You are no wife of mine," he said, and went into the house, into his chamber, locking the door. He opened the Good Book, sought a passage to soothe his mind...

He found none.

14.

Payne and his wife did not exchange words after that; they avoided crossing each other's paths. Payne fed himself. He didn't see his daughter, either, but that did not matter. He was a stranger in this home, *his own home*, purchased by the dirty money of his defiled wife's father. He spent most of his time in town, tending to the congregation, saving their eternal souls from damnation. When people asked of his wife's whereabouts, he said she wasn't feeling well, and opted to stay home with the child. This was not entirely a lie.

Many notions danced (like demons) through Reverend Payne's mind. The first, that there had been no Indian. She had a lover somewhere, some young man from town who came to her when he was gone, and gave her that child; she was lying to him, trying to play at role of victim, trying to win sympathy. Payne looked into every man's face in town, wondering: *Is he my wife's lover? Is he the David to my Bathsheba?* He later ruled this out; what man would be so low as to seduce the wife of a Reverend and risk eternal fires? Anathema, yes: Satan. It all became quite clear now. *This was the work of Satan.* THE DEVIL feared Payne, always had: for wasn't it Payne who saved so many souls in Boston, causing THE DEVIL to possess the men of his church and go against him? Satan had followed him out here, and struck him straight at home. Perhaps there *was* an Indian out in the barn, a shape Satan had taken. It made sense: why would she help such an animal? Like the serpent who had sweet-talked Eve in the Garden, so had this devil-in-Indian-guise do to his wife. Women were such ignorant, gullible creatures, indeed! Satan had beguiled her, *taken* her, placed his wanton seed into her womb to give forth an anti-Christ. It was so damn clear now, and the Reverend knew his mission. The world's fate was in his hands. THE DEVIL would have a son here to rule and destroy the planet as was prophesied in the Book of Revelations. God, he knew now, had chosen him to change the face of the future.

Payne dreamt one night that he came across a burning cacti plant in the desert.

"Tell me my mission," he said, for he knew what the plant was, as did Moses.

"Thou salt not kill," the bush boomed in a large voice.

"I will not break a commandment," Payne avowed, falling to his knees.

He woke, thinking, *I shall not kill....*

THE DEVIL was sitting outside the window—listening to Payne, having watched Payne's dream—and quietly laughing.

15.

When she went into labor, Katherine stumbled from her room, knocking hard on her husband's door; he opened it reluctantly. She was on the floor—water broken, blood at her feet. Reverend Payne refused to fetch the town doctor or take her to him. He helped his wife back to her bed, but this was all he would do. He would let this aberration take its own course. If Satan's child should die due to lack of proper care, so be it. This was out of his hands.

Evangeline woke from the sound of her mother's screams, and began crying herself. Payne ignored both females, watching the birthing with rapt repugnance.

His wife thrashed on the bed, shrieking, spittle flying from her mouth like a bullet-shot coyote in the dirt—back arched, body off the bed. The child slid out from between her legs. Payne gasped. He had expected something with hoofed-feet, horns, a tail—a demon of fitting pretense. No. This was a human child. Brown of skin, green of eyes, and healthy with cry. A boy. *A boy child.* The afterbirth came next, looking more of the thing of nightmares than the Reverend had expected—as well as a flux of blood. Katherine wailed, then fell still, blood pouring around the infant. What was wrong with her? Why was she bleeding so?

"Jedediah," she said.

He looked at her face.

Her glare pierced into him, undiluted, straight to his God-given soul. *"Come here, Jedediah,"* she said.

She knew she was going to die. She felt her insides rupturing, bursting. There wasn't much time left. She could hear the newborn's wails. She saw that it was a boy. He looked beautiful. She beckoned her husband to come to him, her voice weak yet insistent. He moved toward her, and he was frightened. How much of THE DEVIL was still inside her? She reached out and grabbed his wrist. He tried to pull free. Her nails dug in, puncturing flesh.

Blood....

"I'm leaving you now," she said, coughing up her guts, "but you must make a vow."

"Katherine," he said, still trying to free himself.

"No matter what, no matter *what*—you *will not* harm this child. You will not give him away, you will not hurt him, you will not leave him to starve. He is my son, and he is the brother of your daughter."

"Katherine," he said again.

"Swear to this," she said.

He would not.

"SWEAR IT!" she cried. "IF YOU DO NOT, AND IF YOU GO AGAINST YOUR WORD, BY THE *LORD* MY SOUL WILL HAUNT AND TORMENT YOU FOR ALL YOUR YEARS! I MAY GO TO HELL BUT I WILL MAKE A DEAL WITH SATAN TO LET ME HAUNT YOU UNTIL YOU GO MAD!"

He was shaking to near paroxysms. "I swear," he said.

"SWEAR IT TO THAT UNJUST GOD OF YOURS!"

"Blasphemy!" he choked.

"SWEAR!"

"I swear to the Lord, I—I—"

"SWEAR ON THE BIBLE!"

He did.

She let go of him. "Give me my child," she murmured.

He would not do this. He had done enough. Evil was all around him. He began to pray out loud, asking the Angels for exact and swift relief. Katherine strained to grab the child by herself, pull him to her bosom. Blood was everywhere he looked. Payne went to get his daughter, to take her away from this sight. Evangeline was crying for her mother.

The boy child stopped his wailing as soon as Katherine offered him her breast. As the child suckled, she took her last breath.

Reverend Payne returned a few hours later, inquisitive more than concerned. His wife was still, her skin icy cold, the child asleep. Her stiff arms held the demon infant. He pulled the baby free, with abhorrence. The child began to cry. He wanted to smother it on the spot. But he had sworn an oath to her; he'd agreed to abide by God's mandate in the dream. God had His Ways and those Ways were strange, yes, of course, he knew this. Payne had his own motives, however: he had to watch and make sure this child of iniquity did not do the biding of his true sire. If he gave the boy up for adoption, he may fall into the hands of someone who could lead him to a position to destroy the world. No, he would keep Satan's child here, as a prisoner, and make sure he did no detriment to and in the world.

Reverend Jedediah Payne looked down at the brown newborn with green eyes and said, "Your name shall Judas..."

CHAPTER TWO

1.

They were running up the hill—a young boy and girl, holding hands. Her long curly blonde hair flowed back like dreamy ripples in the wind; her pale blue dress offset her pale white skin—a grave contrast to the boy she was with, whose hair was black as night, skin dark and red-brown like clay. The pants the boy wore were too short for him, his shirt soiled and torn. He was a little younger than the girl who happened to be his sister. Evangeline Payne was more than a sister to ten-year-old Judas Payne. She was also a mother, a friend, the only person of the opposite sex that he had ever come into contact with, since his father didn't allow him to go into town, and people seldom came to visit the Payne's homestead.

Judas was losing his breath, hand still in hers. "I'm getting tired, Evangeline! Can't we stop? Here?"

She halted, looking at the clear sky, arms out. Gazing on her face, her glinting eyes, her smile—well, Judas felt an odd warmth inside his heart.

"It's too beautiful out here!" Evangeline said. "The sun is out and the clouds and rain have gone! The baby birds are opening their eyes and singing and *surly*—you take note of my words, little brother—the angels are dancing and rejoicing..." She sighed the sigh of one with purity in the soul : "—for this here is the true beauty of God." She turned to him, reaching out to touch his face with one dainty, frail hand. "Like you, my brother. The proof of the beauty in God. A very angel sent to this earth. I know this in my heart—I know this from my dreams."

She smiled, moving to tickle him. Judas yelped, and they both fell to the grass. Judas was giggling, pleading for her to stop. He began to tickle her in return.

"You talk like Father sometimes," he said, "but without all the anger and spittle. You talk like...poetry."

He wouldn't stop tickling her.

"No!" she cried, her laughter uncontrollable.

They lay still in the grass, reaching to hold hands.

"How can I be beautiful?" Judas asked. "Only girls can be 'beautiful.'"

"Boys *can,*" she assured him, "and *you* are."

Judas blushed at his sister's observation. "No," he could not look at her, "you are the one...the one who is—"

She whispered, "You are an angel, God's angel."

And softer, "Give us a little kiss, angel."

Judas was nervous, as he always was when she wanted to be close. But he kissed her, quickly on the lips.

"Now give us another," she said.

And he did.

2.

They did not return to the house until late, the sun almost down. Evangeline was not concerned but fear made Judas tremble. He knew what was waiting for them when they got to the home of the Reverend—the Reverend who was waiting and, as Judas expected, quite angry. The eldest Payne's face was red with disapproval and rancor. He looked at them both, only quickly, and distastefully; then at Evangeline, without the previous aversion.

"Where *were* you, young woman?"

She said happily, "Just taking in the first glorious hours of God's Springtime, Father."

"I *told* you about staying away *long*, girl. You cause me to worry—"

He glared at Judas, eyes piercing like arrows into soft wood. "Boy, this is your fault— "

"It wasn't any of his fault, Father," Evangeline said quickly, moving away from Judas and going to her father: she was the barrier between the animosity. "Don't start on him," she said, more a statement than a request.

She sounds more and more like her mother, the Reverend thought.

Judas held his breath.

Reverend Payne turned away. "Get yourself in the house and get supper ready," and with a wave in Judas's direction: "*you* get yourself into your barn, boy."

With that, the Reverend walked away.

Judas let out his breath, thankful the confrontation didn't go the way of the Reverend striking him with a large hand, as this man whom he knew as his father was often prone to do. Evangeline turned at him, eyes large and wet; she nodded and then went inside as told.

Judas had never been allowed into the house. The only times he'd been in there was when he could sneak inside as the Reverend was away, doing what he did at the church. Evangeline would let her half-brother in. Other than that, the house was forbidden territory; Judas was not even allowed to have dinner with his family.

He ate what scraps were allotted to him.

In the barn, there was a worn old cot in the far corner. Judas liked to think that some brave Union solider once used the cot to sleep on during the war. There was a book under the cot, one of the many Evangeline would bring to him from time to time. Wrapped in the blanket was a slightly stale piece of bread. Judas' stomach ached; this would have to do for now. He nibbled at the bread, then opened the book. He squinted as he read. The sunlight would be gone soon, and he needed to conserve the oil in the lamp.

He lay down on the cot, read some, closed his eyes, and fell asleep.

The Devil came to him during his dreams. He did not know who The Devil really was—Judas would meet up with a white, red-eyed albino rabbit, a very big rabbit, and the rabbit would tell him: "Love your sister, do as I say."

"I do love her," he'd tell the rabbit, "I always will."

A few hours later, he opened his eyes. Evangeline, in a thick white bedding gown, came in. Her golden hair was pulled back, tied with a blue ribbon. She had a plate with her: meat, vegetables, some beans.

After Reverend Payne went to sleep each night, Evangeline would secretly bring her brother a proper dinner.

Without her, he knew, he would surely be dead now; if not sickly, dumb, and weak.

3.

Judas would read to her. Evangeline liked to hear his voice saying all the pretty words in the books. His sister had taught him how to read, and he read quite well, improving with each year. His voice was unquestionably resplendent, and could make angels weep—this she was sure of. His voice would make her cry, at times, especially when he read something that was particularly sad (one that would always remain in her mind was Nathaniel Hawthorne's *The Scarlet Letter*, a book she'd heard was taboo, but never forbidden by her father, who had no interest in books other than The Holy Bible). Most of the books were a legacy left by their mother, a woman she did not remember; killed, her father claimed, "by that demon child, your brother." Never did she believe Judas was an intentional cause of her mother's death; she'd passed away giving birth to him, yes, but so did many other women these days.

Knowing that, Evangeline Payne had no desire to ever have children.

"You're just sixteen," her brother told her one evening when she informed him of her opinion on the matter, "one day you will want a child."

"Only if it can be your child," Evangeline said, acting like this was a joke, but inside her heart, she was telling the truth.

Each day, over the years, as the two became teenagers, his ability to read to her improved, and he was quite excellent, much better than she; in fact, he read more than she did, staying up many nights with the books, the lantern in the barn. When the books in the house had been depleted, re-read and re-re-read, Evangeline began to borrow books from the small Tyburn Library, or purchase what she could get her hands on, when she had change to spare, and without her father's knowledge and inevitable judgment. Judas devoured anything his sister brought him, whether it was fiction or poetry, historical texts, monographs, the drama of Shakespeare, the philosophy of Plato, or adventure stories of the Civil War and gunfighters of the West.

Although referred to, by his father, as a heathen, a beast, a non-human, and a devil, Judas Payne, absorbing the literature, was obviously not as lacking in intelligence as the Reverend claimed. It's without surprise that in his early teen years, he began to question his father's seeming distaste, in fact hatred, for him, and his position in this so-called "family." Judas was well aware of the marked difference of his skin color compared to his sister's, or even his own father's, and the photos he'd seen of Katherine Payne—she was fair of skin like his sister.

And there was also his unique green eyes...

"He only wants me here to do work," he told his sister once. "I am like a slave."

"That is not true," Evangeline said.

"I've lived all my life in this barn. Why? Why don't I have a room in the house like you?"

"Father is very mysterious," Evangeline said. "As are all men of God."

"I don't believe I am his son," Judas said.

"Of course you are. We have the same mother."

"We are different."

"You are different because you are an angel sent to earth,"

his sister told him, touching his face lightly with her fingernails. He closed his eyes. "You left God's bosom to come here, you have a mission, I know this in my heart," she told him, her lips at his ears, and then at his own lips.

His sister had always looked upon the world with such simplicity, and Judas wanted to protect that innocence. The more he read, the more cynical and bleak he became. One day darkness would fall, he felt this in his bones, to his very young core.

He didn't, however, know how close that day actually was.

4.

It's hard to say whether or not Evangeline Payne was truly aware of the forbidden nature of her feelings for her brother. Naiveté has its blindness, and Evangeline looked upon every thing, every person, with the love of God, and the ignorance of the world.

She did know that her father would vehemently disapprove of the special relationship she had with her brother, and her brother knew this even more; so they took precautions to keep their time together a secret from the pious Reverend.

It's also hard to say whether or not young Judas Payne was truly aware of the forbidden nature of his feelings for his half-sister. He wasn't a young man of the world, after all; and in fact knew very little of the world, except for what he read.

There was no doubt about his feelings, in his mind and heart, the night he had the dazzling dream about her.

It was phenomenal, yes, but also very frightening.

In his dream, they were in a garden, a garden so perfect and wonderful that it was beyond his description, even to himself. Lush trees and plants, fruit everywhere, rivers and lakes, happy animals running about in glee, without fear of hunters or predators. He came upon his sister wading naked in a lake; in fact, she was bathing, using the petals of unnaturally large roses to cleanse her glistening body. She was not startled when he approached her. She smiled at him. She held out her hand, her naked bosoms exposed. "Come in the water with me, Judas," she said, her voice like a song.

He was then amazed, flabbergasted, and terrified of the fact that he was suddenly naked himself. He was not ashamed. Evangeline was goading him to come into the lake. She was splashing the water about her, giggling and joyous.

He jumped into the water. It was warm and very clean. He laughed and felt very light and perfect. He swam toward her.

He stood facing his sister.

"Give me a kiss," she said.

They kissed, so lightly.

"Hold me tight," she said.

Their bodies, in the lake, pressed together; there was nothing under their feet. They were no longer in the water, but in the sky, floating—no, *flying,* naked body to naked body.

"We are man and wife," Evangeline said.

They started to fall.

They screamed.

They hit the ground.

Judas Payne woke up, shrieking. It took him a moment to realize he'd been dreaming. His heart was racing; he was, regardless, terrified. There was a weird sensation in his crotch. He examined himself, to find that there was a sticky, smelly white fluid down there.

5.

His dream, a few weeks later, would prove to have prophetic properties.

The Reverend was in town, attending to both a funeral and a wedding. Judas knew his father would not return until late at night, as he often did when this duty called him. Evangeline was in the house. From the barn, he stared at the house. He could heart her moving in there, could almost smell her. It wasn't the smell of food in the kitchen, which he had always been able to detect since he was a child, since his tenure inside the barn, *but he could smell her body*—the freshness of it, the excitement of it.

She would come to him, he knew this. She always did, and often early, when the Reverend was away. However, this time he could not wait for her. Something odd and powerful compelled him to act—something that, in the material he read, was often described as an "unseen force."

He went into the house, the forbidden land, this time on his own, without the guidance and acknowledgment of his beautiful sibling. He almost stopped himself at the entrance, like there was an invisible barrier, like he was an devil at the Gates of Heaven.

He could hear her in the house, somewhere. He was sure of this. He could smell her, and he could see her—she was naked, just like the dream, maybe there was even a lake in here.

She was singing.

He knew that voice very well—so soft, so perfect, so drawing—

"Evangeline," he said.

6.

"Judas," she said.

Evangeline Payne found herself not at all surprised that her brother had been watching her bathing in the metal tub, almost as if she'd known that one day, *some* day, this day would come. She'd been humming a tune, running the soap over her body, and she turned her head, and she saw him at the door, his green eyes blaring like something outside of this world. Her heart jumped—yes—and for a brief moment she was scared—*yes*—but this was her beloved angel, her messenger from God, and she knew she had nothing to fear.

She inquired, "How long have you been standing there, my angel on earth?"

"Not long," he confessed.

"Why," she asked next, "are you here?"

"I'm not sure," he said. "I was driven. Forgive me, please."

He turned to go. She rose from the tub, like the goddess she was, and said, "Judas, no, do not leave me."

He stopped.

"Come here."

He couldn't move. He *would* not move. He was petrified. Water flowed in rivets down her body, soap clung to her in patchy spots. Her nipples were pink, her breasts pointed and small, the hair between her legs golden and thick.

"Judas," she said.

"No!" he cried, and turned. He ran out of the house—this den of danger and estrangement—and returned to the only home he knew: the barn. He lay on his cot and there were tears in his eyes.

His body was on fire and he didn't like this sensation at all.

Not long after, she came to him. He knew she would. He was still face-down on the cot.

"Judas Payne," his sister said.

"Yes," he replied.

"I brought you some food."

He turned around. She was wearing a flowing blue night-gown, her hair done up. She was holding a plate of vegetables. She smiled, not a hint of anger or judgment on her face or in her eyes. He was sure she would be angry with him, but was relieved—and felt warm all over his body—that she was not.

She sat next to him.

"Are you hungry?" she asked.

"Not for food," he told her.

"What do you mean by that?"

"I do not know."

"Tell me," she said.

"I feel hungry for something," Judas said. "My soul feels hungry. Is that possible? Can a soul be hungry?"

"Of course," Evangeline said. "The soul is always hungry. It is hungry for God, and other things."

"What other things?"

"Love."

"Isn't God love?"

"Yes," she said. "But love is so much more, don't you think?"

"I think so," he said.

"Are you hungry for me?" his sister asked him.

He didn't know what to say.

"I am hungry for you," she told him.

He didn't know what she meant. He was shaking. She made him feel more at ease by taking a carrot from the plate and biting into it. He took a piece of celery. They both laughed, which broke the tension.

"Would you like me to read to you?" he said.

"Yes, but not right now. Right now, I would like to lie down next to you. I would like to feel you next to me. I would like to put my head on your chest and feel your heartbeat. Can I do that?"

"I suppose so," the young Judas said, feeling frightened again.

Evangeline was in control, and she let him know this. She put the plate down on the floor and a hand on his chest, pushing him back on the cot. She lay next to him, cuddled into him, her head on his chest, just as she said it would be. This wasn't the first time they had been like this, of course, but it seemed different and new to Judas.

They were quiet for a long time. He listened to her breath. He thought she might be asleep. Her eyes were opened.

"You saw me naked," she said.

"Forgive me," he said.

"What is there to forgive?"

"I went into the house. I snuck in like a thief."

"Why did you do that?"

"I do not know," he said.

"Yes you do."

"I do not," he said.

"It's all right," she said.

"THE DEVIL came over me," Judas said, and: "THE DEVIL was inside me, *making* me do things I did not want or mean."

She laughed and said, "You sound like father!"

He laughed too. He reached out to touch her.

"Did you like seeing me naked?" she asked her brother.

"Yes," he replied.

They did not speak anymore. This time, she did fall asleep in his arms; and soon, he was asleep as well.

He next found her jumping up, grabbing the plate.

"Father will be home soon!"

"Go inside, fast," he said.

"Goodnight, my angel on Earth," she said.

"Goodnight," he said.

My love, he thought.

7.

As it turned out, they didn't talk about that night, and resumed their lives as sister and outcast brother as they had before. When she came to see him in the barn, bringing him food, he would read to her from the latest book, and then she would depart. Within a few weeks, Judas Payne began to believe the whole incident—seeing her in the tub, holding her on the cot—was merely a dream.

8.

And so it was like a dream that, when the Reverend was away in town for a whole day, Evangeline came to him in the barn and asked him if he would help her bathe.

He didn't understand.

She said, "I will place my body in the tub, and you will help to clean my body."

His sister held out her hand. He took it. She lead him to the house. At the door, he became frightened. His body was hot, his heart beat fast, his legs were giving out from under him—

"I can't," he said.

"Pardon me?"

He started to cry. "I CAN'T!"

He ran back into the barn, where it was safe.

Evangeline didn't immediately go after him, as he thought she might—as he hoped she might. Instead, she came to him several hours later. Her skin was glowing and radiant. She'd taken her bath. She sat next to him on his cot and looked troubled.

"You don't love me," she said.

"How can you say that?"

"You ran from my gesture of love."

"I'm afraid."

"Of father? He's far away."

"I'm afraid of..." he started, and realized he didn't know the words to express what was inside his hell-bound heart.

So he said, "I just am."

"Of me?" she asked in a small voice.

He was horrified by her accusation.

"No! *No,*" he said.

They stood there, staring at one another.

"Last time," she said, "you told me you liked to see me naked."

"I saw you that *one* time," he said.

"And?"

"Why," he inquired with pain, "are you tormenting me?"

Evangeline burst into tears and ran back into the house. Judas started for her, but that unseen hand stopped him. He could hear her in the house, sobbing and saying his name with disgust.

In the barn, he pounded his head against the wood. He did this so many times, and so strongly, that he bled.

9.

The next night, Evangeline brought him food and acted like nothing had happened. He ate, she watched.

She touched his hair.

She said, "My angel."

She asked him to read to her.

She handed him a book.

Judas read to her. They lay on his cot, as they always did, her head near his chest.

"It is a warm night," Evangeline said, softly, "a very *warm* night."

They were both sweating, but the weather wasn't the only reason. There was something unsaid between these two young people. Evangeline got up, and began to remove her dress.

"What are you doing?" he said, feeling the familiar fear.

The girl held her brother's gaze. She didn't take her eyes off him. "You *like* to see me naked, and I want you to see me naked," she told him. "So you shall. And if you run from me, I will scream."

He was too aghast to even think about running, or moving, observing his sister disrobe. Her dress dropped at her feet, and she was as nude as the day she was born.

"This is *me*, Judas," she said.

He opened his mouth.

Tears were at her eyes.

"Do you *know* what is in my heart?" she asked.

He said, honestly, "No."

"But you *should.*"

"Do you know," he said, straining each word, "what is in *my* heart?"

"Yes," she said.

"No, you don't," he said.

"I want to," she said.

"No," he said.

"Can I lay with you?" Evangeline Payne said. "Will you still read to me?"

He nodded. She went to him. He thought he might explode. They were on the cot, her naked body against his. Judas tried to read, but he couldn't. He told her this. He said, "I can't. *How can I?"*

"Take your clothes off," she said. There was something strange in her eyes; for a moment, she didn't look or act like the girl he'd known all his life. "Let's be naked next to each other, just like Adam and Eve," he said.

He gave into her will. There was much in him that wanted to comply, that wanted to do this. He knew nothing of sex, or men and women, of procreation, other than the part in the beginning of the Bible when Adam and Eve discovered they had shame by each other's nakedness after eating The Fruit. He'd never understood that part (and, in fact, didn't understand much of the Bible); now, however, he did. Evangeline helped him out of his clothes. Standing nude before her nakedness, he *did* feel shame, and he didn't know where these strong emotions came from. He didn't like this at all. He moved his hands to cover himself.

Evangeline had the same sense of opprobrium, and also hid parts of her body with her arms and hands. She quickly moved to the oil lamp, and diminished the light. They were in darkness.

She moved toward Judas. He felt the heat of her body close to his.

She said, "Let's lie down next to each other. I want to feel your skin against my skin."

She pushed him back on the cot, on his back. She lay next to him, her head on his chest. This time was so much different than before. Judas felt the stirring in his groin. His sex organ was hard, like when he awoke from those dreams which he was having more frequently.

"You're shaking," she said.

"No."

"Yes you are. Are you cold?"

"No," he said.

"Are you scared?"

"Yes," he said.

She said, "Don't be."

"Aren't you scared?" he asked.

"I was," she said. "But I'm not anymore. This feels so right, so perfect. I can smell you like I never have before."

"You have read about this in books," Judas said after a while. "You have read about men and women doing this."

She said, "Yes."

"Where did you get such a book?"

"I found it hidden in the house, with others."

"Father has such books?"

"Yes," she said.

"Does he read them?"

"They had the names of people from town written in the front pages, in his writing," she told him. "I think he took them from these people."

"Bad books," Judas said.

"They aren't so bad."

"Why does he have them?"

"When it comes to father," she said, "why ever ask a question?"

They both laughed at that, and it seemed to make things better.

10.

For several weeks, almost every night, when Evangeline felt it safe to come to him, they lay naked together in the barn. Their hands began to explore each other's bodies, cautiously, gently, with much fear.

It was inevitable that the Reverend Jedediah Payne would discover this, and such a discovery would have a negative, rippling effects in Biblical proportions. It was his discovery of the siblings' affection for one another that set each young person on the painful course of their lives for many years to come. Indeed, both Judas and Evangeline Payne would, later in the future, look back on this night and wonder how their lives would be different had not the following events took place.

Neither brother nor sister ever had the notion that the Reverend would come into the barn at night, for he never had in the past, all these years. He often avoided the barn as much as he could, certainly when Judas was there; and when the Reverend retired for the night, he slept deeply, and hardly ever came out of his bedroom.

It was the dream Reverend Payne was having that took him to the barn. In his dream, he was older, and so was Judas. Payne was in a dark room, praying to the Lord, when Judas appeared, a gun—or was it a knife?—in his hand. "How dare you step foot in this place of the Lord, devil boy," the Reverend said, and Judas replied: "I am here to kill you, Father," and the devil boy did just that: he killed Payne, in front of *God* he *murdered* the Reverend, and there were many screams, like the dead from Hell in chorus. The Reverend was shot—or stabbed—in the heart, and the pain and surprise was tremendous.

He woke up clutching at his chest, like a terrified woman (he thought). He was disoriented. It took him close to a minute to understand that he had been dreaming, and he was alive and well. The Reverend was relieved, and angry. Why would such a dream come to him? Was God trying to tell him something? Was that devil boy sending evil thoughts his way, invading his sleep and peace? The boy was almost a man now, and if he were harboring thoughts of ill will, if ideas of murder were in his heart—

An image came to the Reverend: Judas in the barn, in a pentagram, in candlelight, performing some sort of ritual to his true maker, Satan—

He was going to find out what that boy was doing, maybe have a talk with him—

Reverend Payne put on a coat, lit an oil lamp, and went out to the barn.

What he saw—the two children naked in each other's arms—was the last thing on God's world he expected...

11.

"DEVIL!"

Evangeline Payne squealed when she heard her father's voice, and saw him standing at the entrance of the barn. She quickly moved away from her brother, to the floor, finding her nightclothes and covering the shame of her young body, which the Reverend had never seen.

In fact, it was the brief glimpse of his daughter's bareness that caused Payne to stop, to consider her. *Good Lord*, he thought, *she is a beautiful creature, full of lust and sin—*

Judas Payne was struggling to put his pants on.

"What," the Reverend said, "have you done to my daughter, you devil child?"

Evangeline was crying. "Father—"

"SHUT UP HARLOT!"

Judas was looking for his shirt.

"First you kill my wife, and now ruin my daughter," the Reverend said, stepping forward, "and you desire to murder me."

"Nothing bad has happened, Father," Evangeline said.

The Reverend was slowly becoming furious. "You have carnal knowledge with this creature, and you say nothing bad has happened? Has he also poisoned your mind, girl?!?"

"I have had no knowledge with him," she said.

"He is Satan!" the Reverend cried. "He has ruined you and will murder me! The vow I made to my departed Katherine is lifted! This is a battle between good and evil and God is on my side and I shall prevail!"

With that, the Reverend lunged at the boy. Judas looked up. His father was swinging the oil lamp in the air. Before Judas could move away, he was struck in the face by the lamp. The light went out, and it was dark again in the barn. Judas heard Evangeline scream when the lamp hit on his face. The glass shattered. His face was wet and hot. He had oil on him, and something else. He tasted it in his mouth, dripping down: blood.

Judas stumbled back. He touched his face, and felt the shard of glass that was embedded in his right eye.

"Where are you, devil boy?" the Reverend said in the dark.

Moonlight came into the barn from the opened entrance. The Reverend was lurching his way, large hands out. *He'll strangle me to death,* Judas thought. Evangeline was still screaming, crying, on the barn floor, clutching her nightclothes to herself.

Judas saw, from his left eye, the ax leaning against the wall. He quickly grabbed it, turned around and brought it up with both hands, blood seeping out of his right eye, the pain finally reaching him, the pain vast and indescribable. The Reverend charged. Judas brought the ax down, hard as he could, and jumped out of the way.

The caterwaul that came from the Reverend's mouth was like nothing neither Judas nor Evangeline—or even the Reverend himself—had ever heard. It did not sound human. The ax blade had deeply embedded itself into the Reverend's upper left arm.

Jedediah Payne fell to the ground, trying to pull the ax free from his flesh.

Everyone was breathing hard, each of the three with their individual sounds of pain and fear.

"You shall pay dearly!" the Reverend was saying.

"Judas," Evangeline said, "run."

Judas didn't know what to do. He couldn't move his legs. He reached for his face and pulled the shard of glass from his eye. It didn't hurt as much as he expected. He was bleeding a lot.

"Run, Judas, run away," his sister was saying. "He'll kill you." It was too dark for her to see the injury her brother had suffered.

"He'll kill us both," Judas said.

"She is right," the Reverend said. "I shall kill you, and God will help me." He'd managed to remove the ax, but he was too weak to stand, losing so much blood.

Judas knew he had to run. He found his shirt and shoes and picked them up. He moved toward the entrance.

Evangeline was putting her night clothes on. "Hurry," she

said, "go now."

He nodded.

"I love you, angel," she said.

He ran into the night.

12.

Reverend Payne was drifting in and out of consciousness, lying on the barn floor and bleeding. His soiled daughter was looking down at him.

"Don't try to move, Father," she said. "You're badly hurt. I'll try to tie something on your arm and stop the bleeding. Then I'll go into town and fetch Doc Kelly."

"No," he said. "I will bleed to death by the time you return. Listen to me, girl, listen to me: I'll tell you what you must do."

"Tell me, Father."

"Build a fire in here, quickly. Take a piece of wood, and let it burn at the end. When it is hot, you must put the burning end to where I'm bleeding. This will cauterize the artery." He wasn't speaking from experience. He knew enough basic anatomy to know that a major vein was bleeding, and cutting off the circulation would not help. He knew about cauterization from what he'd heard about injuries in the War.

"I don't know if I can do that," she said, softly. She was scared.

"Then I will die," her father said, "and my death will be on your conscience, and surely you will go to Hell."

Evangeline made a fire out of wood and hay in the barn, using matches from the house. If the barn burns down, she thought, so be it. She put a long piece of wood in the flame.

"Do it now," her father said weakly.

She stuck the end of the burning wood to his wound, and again the Reverend made that same inhuman shriek as he had before—it curdled her blood and froze her skin. The Reverend passed out. She thought, for a moment, that he was dead. She inspected him against the light of the fire. The flesh at his wound was dark, smoldering, and stank, but the bleeding seemed to have stopped. She touched his chest and felt his heartbeat. She wasn't sure if she was relieved or disappointed. The fire she'd made was getting bigger, spreading around the hay. She grabbed the blanket from her brother's cot and threw it over the fire, stamping it out. The barn went dark again, like her heart. She was worried about Judas.

13.

Judas was worried too—for himself, for his sister, for the future in general. He ran and ran in the night, through the empty fields and hills, going northwest, away from town. He occasionally stopped and caught his breath. The bleeding at his eye had stopped, but it was swollen shut, and he knew his eye was badly damaged. If he had the energy, he would stop and cry. But he had to keep running. If he'd killed the Reverend, the law would come after him. The law would come after him anyway, because he had injured his father, and despite his own wound, he knew the law would take the side of a man of God instead of a boy like him.

After a few hours, he could run no more. His legs hurt, his body hurt, and his head was throbbing. He lay on the ground and looked up at the stars with his one good eye.

Take me, God, he thought. *I don't want to live this way...*

14.

Evangeline Payne returned to her home late in the morning with Doc Kelly. She'd explained to the doctor what happened, he nodded, and gathered what he needed in his bag and took to the Reverend's house with the girl by horse and buggy. The Doctor was a robust man in his fifties, handsome in a rugged way, Evangeline thought. She considered him as she sat next to him on the ride home. She knew the Doctor was a widow, and she considered the idea of having him as her husband. She knew very well that she would have to find a man to marry her and take her in soon, for surely she could not live with her father anymore. If not the Doctor, *someone*—she had to entertain alternatives for her future, a future without her brother.

She half-hoped they would discover the Reverend dead. But he wasn't. He was where she had left him in the barn; his eyes were open.

"Reverend Payne," Doc Kelly said, kneeling down to inspect the wound.

"Doctor," Payne said.

"This looks bad."

"I imagine."

"I can help you," Doc Kelly said, "but you're going to have to lose the arm."

"Reckoned such."

Kelly turned to get his bag. He saw the girl standing by the barn.

"Perhaps you should wait in the house," Kelly said.

CHAPTER THREE

1.

Judas Payne was aware of motion. He was lying down on blankets. He was rattling back and forth. He'd been having a dream that he was on a boat, a schooner perhaps, the kind he'd read about in one of the books his sister had brought to him years ago. He was on a grand adventure in this dream, that was for sure; he was scared too, and riding the waves, trying to get away from red serpents—giant creatures—emerging out of the water. His father was riding one of the serpents, clinging to its scaly neck with one hand, holding up an oil lamp with the other. "Devil boy!" his father kept yelling, "we'll get you yet! We'll rid the world of you yet!"

But he wasn't on a boat in the seas, or on an adventure. He realized he was lying in the back of a covered wagon, and there were bandages on his face—well, around his injured eye. It all came back to him now, the night, the violence. He was terri-fied—where was he? Was the sheriff carting him back to jail, and undoubtedly a certain public hanging?

A young woman was peering down at him. She wasn't much older than Evangeline, with a plain but pleasant round face, dirty blonde hair pulled back in a bun. "You're awake, finally," she said. "You've been unconscious for two days. I was begin-ning to worry about you."

He tried to sit up. She put a hand on his chest and shook her head. Her nice face made him feel a little at ease—just a little.

"Don't be afraid," she said.

"I'm not."

"And don't lie. Lying is a sin."

"So my father tells me. I am afraid," he confessed. "Where am I?"

"On the road to a great adventure!" she said gleefully.

Judas thought he might have been talking in his sleep, about seas and serpents and quests.

"My name is Mary Jo Scroggins," she told him.

"Judas," he said. "Payne."

"Judas Payne?"

"Yes, ma'am."

"Quite a name."

"So is yours."

"My name is plain as day," she said, "just like my looks, eh? I'm your average, hard-working girl hoping for a bright future for my family. Well, my family is just my husband and me, Robert Kevin Scroggins, who is, right now, manning two horses pulling this buggy, but we're planning on many, *many* children—but give us time," she giggled, "we've only been married a few months.

"He'll be happy to know that you're all right, Mr. Payne. We found you lying on the ground on the trail. Thought you were dead. Almost got yourself runned over and killed." Her voice became somber. "You had a nasty piece of glass wedged in your eye. Count your blessings I've had some nursing experience—not much, mind you, but enough so that I could remove that shard. And we had to take your eye out, too, it was rotting. I'm afraid—"

"I only have one eye," Judas said. He'd already realized this, but her confirmation made the agony worse.

She seemed hurt, looking at him. "I'm sorry. There was nothing I could do. Nothing I knew what to do. Like I said, I've had some nursing experience, but I ain't no doctor and we don't have no doctor in this caravan."

He said, "Caravan?"

"Yes," Mary Jo Scroggins said. "There's eleven wagons. We're on the Santa Fe Trail."

"I—" He didn't know what to say.

"We couldn't leave you," she said. "I couldn't. Robert agreed. But we could let you off, if you need to get back."

"No," he said. "No, I don't need to get back."

"I didn't think so."

"I have nowhere to go."

"I thought so. You can come with us, if you like."

"Where?"

"Why do you think they call it the Santa Fe Trail?" She laughed. He liked her laugh—it was soothing.

"Of course," he said, feeling weak.

She touched his forehead. Her palm was dry. "You need to sleep more. We'll be stopping to camp in a few hours, as it gets dark, and making dinner."

Sleep came quickly and easily.

2.

He was awake in time for dinner. There were indeed eleven covered wagons in this procession, each with a family of men and women in their late teens or early twenties, some with children and some, like the Scrogginses, not. They were a healthy, hardy, good-natured group of people who'd begun this journey from Independence and Franklin, Missouri, all with the Southwest and the start of a life on their minds.

Robert Kevin Scroggins had a firm grip when he shook hands with Judas; a wide smile and a joyful glint in his eye. He was a short but thick-chest man, strong in body and spirit, so it seemed. "Thank the Lord that you are alive well," Scroggins said, "however..."

"One eye is better than none," Judas said, trying to be humorous. He failed, since Scroggins' expression was grave.

Judas realized that he hadn't yet come to terms with the fact that he was going to lead the rest of his life blind in one eye.

He would be a freak...

People would look at him...

Judas wasn't even sure what kind of life he had to look forward to, so it didn't really seem to matter at the moment.

For the moment, he was hungry, and food was being cooked at the campfire.

Scroggins put his arm around Judas' shoulders. "You're a fine man, I can tell. You'll get through this. Believe that the Lord has a path for all, however queer it may be. Are you hungry?"

"Very."

"Come, let's eat. My wife tells me you're going to join us on our trip."

"I suppose I am," Judas said.

"Good," Scroggins said, "good."

Dinner consisted of baked beans and bread. Judas was ravished. Eating quickly, he wondered what Evangeline was doing, he wondered what was going on back at home. Thinking these things, his stomach knotted. He made himself not think these things. That life was over, lost like his eye.

He was surprised that none of the others questioned him. They didn't ask why he'd been found on their trail unconscious and injured, what he'd done, where he even came from. Everyone was pleasant, concerned for his well-being, and delighted that he was enjoying his meal so much, for such simple food.

It may come to a surprise as well, that (as Judas Payne would later reflect) no one questioned the dark color of his skin, for he was obviously not a white person, as they all were. The Indian in his features stood out, and some could have, and would later, mistaken him for Mexican, until they heard him speak with a Kansas twang. It should be noted that in this Santa Fe Trail caravan was a new breed of young people, non-judgmental, righteous but not pious, looking to get away from the world created by their forefathers, with the shadow of the Civil War— while long gone since they were children—still looming.

But good people come to terrible ends, as Judas Payne would learn throughout his life. Evil sought out the good in America, to tear apart and consume. The lessons that made Judas Payne the man he would become started here.

3.

Evangeline Payne was a ghost in her own house. She remained in her room most of the time, until her Father left; even then, sometimes she did not come out, except to get a bite to eat. There was nothing here for her anymore. Her brother was gone; there was not only a great emptiness in her life, but in her heart and soul. If she didn't know how much her brother meant to her before—how much she dearly adored him—then she did now. Not knowing if he was alive or dead beguiled her the most. Reverend Payne did not tell either Doc Kelly or Sheriff Lish the truth, and she wasn't surprised by her father's lying—all the hypocrisies and deceptions of the man were now quite clear to her. The Reverend said that a bandit, a hoodlum, a "thief in the night" had come onto his land with the intent of robbery and to "defile my young daughter." The Reverend had confronted this foul man, and in the struggle, the man had used the ax on the Reverend, and fled. When Sheriff Lish asked Evangeline if this were true, she looked down and didn't say a word to the contrary—she could feel the Reverend glaring at her, forbidding her not to speak.

"Miss Payne?" the Sheriff said.

"She is frightened," the Reverend declared, "and ashamed."

"It took a lot of courage for this young lady to ride into town and get me," Doc Kelly said. "She should be commended."

"We shouldn't bother the poor girl with this," Sheriff Lish said, clearing his throat. "What did this outlaw look like?" he asked Jedediah Payne.

The Reverend described a young man much like Judas— dark-skinned, thin with wiry muscles, but: "And eyes as black and evil as the night."

"Prolly Mexican," Lish said.

"I reckon so," the Reverend said.

That night, he was at her door, but she would not unlock it. "Go away, Father," she said.

His voice was soft and ominous, as if his mouth were pressed against the wood on the other side. "Listen to me, girl," he said, "listen to me, you whore of Babylon. No one ever knew about the devil boy staying here, no one knew that he was your half-brother. I made a vow to your mother on her deathbed. I know now that you are truly your mother's daughter. Your mother laid with a monster, and that boy was the product. And you too had the desire to lay with the demon. You are tainted now. You are going to burn in Hell. God and Jesus have turned their faces away from you, you are so foul and filthy. But I tell you this: never utter a word to anyone the truth about that Judas boy. I'm sure he is dead and back in Hell where he belongs. One day, you will meet him in hell, and your foul souls can fornicate in the fiery pits, as you did in the flesh."

She wanted to yell at him, tell him that nothing improper had occurred, that she was not ruined as he believed. But she didn't care what he thought. He was no longer her father. She no longer wanted to live here.

What was she going to do, what was she going to do? She knew she had to find a husband to get away, that was the choice. She was beyond the age to marry. She was seventeen. Again, she thought about Doc Kelly. Perhaps she could go into town and visit him. But to go into town, she's have to leave her room; if she left when the Reverend was here, he might confront her, tell her awful things—and if she went into town when he was there, she might see him, walking down the street, displaying his missing arm—his stump—like it was a proud badge in his holy—his fictitious—battle against the forces of darkness.

Evangeline never thought about Sheriff Lish as a possible husband, but the Sheriff was thinking of her. He'd never really seen much of the Reverend's daughter when she was in town, but going out to the Payne's land, he was struck by how beautiful she was. Sheriff Lish had been married before, when he was younger, but his beloved first wife had died of the cancer.

There'd been women later, who had some interest, but mostly the Sheriff took to visiting the whores in the neighboring town, Hand (there were no saloons or brothels in Tyburn). That satisfied him enough—at least, the momentary urge of the body, but certainly not the heart, and a man's need for a companion. He was thirty-eight years old and his hair was beginning to gray and he wondered if, truly, a seventeen-year-old daughter of a preacher would be interested in him.

Sheriff Lish knew something wasn't right about the story the Reverend gave him. Over the years, Lish had heard Payne hired the occasional hand to help out, probably transient Mexicans or ruffians; some had said they'd seen some young dark-skinned men working at Payne's home. It was just talk Lish had heard from time to time that meant nothing. Now, however, Lish wondered if the attacker wasn't one of the workers the Reverend employed—and he certainly couldn't fault some wayward young man wanting to ravish a beauty like Evangeline Payne, wrong as it may be.

It was of little consequence, but it gave Sheriff Lish an excuse to go out to the house when the Reverend was in town. He could talk to the girl about the incident, and maybe get to know her better, determine by her reactions if there was any possibility for romance. Or matrimony.

I'm an old fool, Lish thought as he rode out to the Payne's land.

Arriving, he tied his horse near the barn and knocked on the door.

"Hello?" he said. "Is anyone home? Miss Payne?"

Evangeline was there. She was getting some food—what little her stomach could hold these days—and was startled when the Sheriff rode in. They rarely got visitors, and certainly not from a lawman. She was scared. Was the Sheriff here about Judas? Did they catch him? Did they find out the truth?

The truth, that could make her laugh. And why should she be afraid of it? The *truth* was, it was her father who provoked the fight; he attacked Judas first. Judas was only trying to defend himself.

I should fear nothing, she told herself.

"Miss Payne? It's Sheriff Lish, from town."

She took in a deep breath.

"Hello?" the man said.

Just as he was about to give up, Evangeline appeared at the door. She was wearing a simple dress and her hair was messy, but his heart felt warm when seeing her. He just wanted to take her in his arms and....

"Yes, Sheriff?"

"Good day, Miss Payne," and he took off his hat, smiling sheepishly. "We met about three weeks ago—"

"Yes," she said, "I don't have a faulty memory."

"Of course! I didn't mean—well, everything was—"

"Would you like to come inside, Sheriff?"

"Thank you, ma'am. Thank you."

She held the door open. He walked in.

"Can I get you something to eat or drink?" she asked.

"Well, um," he said. "No, thank you, ma'am."

"My father," she said, choking on the words, "is not here."

"Yes, I know. I didn't come here to talk to him."

"Oh?"

"I came here. Well, I came here to see how you are. You certainly must've been quite terrified and troubled by what happened..."

"Yes," she said flatly.

"I just...."

"I'm quite fine, Sheriff," she lied. "Thank you."

"I'm sorry to say we have no leads on the villainous culprit that attacked you and maimed your father."

"That is a shame."

"Yes it is."

"Yes," she said, looking away.

"I'm just so sorry that it happened," he said.

"I am as well."

Awkwardly, Lish said, "Kinda makes me feel like I'm not

doing my job, protecting the people 'round here."

"Well, you cannot be everywhere at once."

"I reckon not."

"Are you sure you wouldn't like a glass of water?"

"Water would be nice, actually. Thank you, ma'am."

She went to get the Sheriff a glass of water. She was glad to be out of the same room with him. She wanted to scream. She composed herself. There were a number of jugs of water in the kitchen, warm and from the well. Judas had retrieved this water from the well.

She returned with the glass of water.

"Thank you, ma'am," Lish said.

"You're welcome. It's a long ride out." She added, "Just to see how I am."

"There's something else."

"I figured there was, Sheriff."

"I was wondering if maybe the ruffian in question was someone your father had hired before."

"What do you mean?" she said. It was like she'd left her body: she was watching herself talk to the man. She was not in her body, but floating on the ceiling.

Sheriff Lish said, "Your father has hired transient workers for this land in the past?"

He had, and these men had worked alongside her brother. But her brother was the one who did most of the work. She felt tears swelling up.

"Yes," she said.

"Was it one of them?"

"No," she said, and then it all came out, she couldn't help herself, she began to sob uncontrollably—for the loss of her beloved, and her life, and her trust in the Reverend, and her trust in God. She tried to stop herself, knowing how unbecoming and embarrassing it was to cry like this in front of a total stranger, but she could not stop.

Sheriff Lish was embarrassed as well. This was so sudden— the girl was calm and poised, refined and elegant, and suddenly she was hysterical with tears. It pained him too see the young woman in this poor condition. He didn't know what to do. She just looked at him, balling. He did what he thought was natural—he moved to hold her, to help her—

Evangeline fell in his embrace. She needed this—to cry into his chest, to cling onto him. He smelled strong, that man smell, and it wasn't bad; it didn't remind her of Judas, but it triggered something soft in her. All men were different, she supposed.

Lish was telling her to hush, that it was all right. He touched her hair.

She wanted to tell him it was *not all right*.

"I'm here," he was saying, "I won't let anyone hurt you."

What was he talking about?

She glanced up at him, and he was looking at her. She knew that look in his eye, she'd seen it in her brother's. She closed her own eyes. She then realize that the Sheriff was trying to kiss her.

She let him. She kissed the man, eyes still closed, pretending the whole while he was Judas...

Ten minutes later, the Sheriff left, feeling good, feeling positive about life. He'd marry this girl after all, that was his goal.

4.

While that was going on in Tyburn, the caravan on the Santa Fe Trail crossed into New Mexico, where they met up with unfortunate and detrimental circumstances.

They were attacked by a band of marauders, as the old saying goes. They were white men, ex-soldiers, twelve of them led by a man known as Colonel Charles K. Jodzio.

Judas Payne was sitting up front in the wagon, next to Robert Scroggins, when Jodzio and his men attacked. The caravan didn't put up much of a fight. They circled the wagons, but the attackers were excellent shots—they didn't kill anyone, they just shot a few men in the shoulders or arms.

Colonel Jodzio didn't want any casualties. He needed live

bodies. His men gathered the families together, separating the men from the women, allowing the children to stay with their mothers.

"I thought if we'd be attacked," Robert Scroggins said softly to Judas, "it would be by Indians. Not our own kind."

The Colonel didn't wear a military uniform, although he had served in the Union during the War and seen many battles. He walked like a solider, with that arrogant stance, and carried a saber on his hip. His men surrounded the captives with rifles and pistols, grinning. They were a dirty, unshaven, smelly bunch that Judas Payne knew were up to no good.

"I am Colonel Charles K. Jodzio!" the man's voice boomed with authority and terror. "Who among you is the leader of this horde?"

Everyone from the caravan looked at each other.

Robert Scroggins stepped forward. "I speak for us."

"And your name?"

"Robert Kevin Scroggins."

"A fine name. We share the same middle name, sir."

"Thank you," Robert said cordially. "Why have you attacked us? Why do you hold us captive?"

Jodzio approached Robert, and stood face to face. "I like a man who gets to the point. All you fine, young, healthy and strong people are now in my employ."

The Colonel's men laughed at that. So did the Colonel, who stepped back, and looked at his prisoners.

"To put it another way," Jodzio said, "you have now become members of a small demographic group known as forced labor. You will be taken to my silver mines, and work those mines, and make me and my men quite rich. We can't do the job ourselves, and we can't afford to hire labor at this time, that will surly cut deep into our profits. In the end, you will be compensated, for I am not a completely cruel man. I can be fair, as you will come to understand—and even appreciate."

"You call yourself a Colonel?" Robert asked.

Jodzio's eyes narrowed, "Yes, I do."

"With what army?"

"I'm retired from the services of our country," Jodzio said. "I got so used to being called Colonel that my men here still do, and I am partial to that title."

"You fought against the South?" Robert said.

"And killed many."

"Then how can you condone slavery such as your propose, sir?"

The Colonel laughed, and his men joined in. "If you believe that we were in that bloody and glorious war to free niggers, you're sorely mistaken, young man. I could care less about niggers. I have niggers at the mine. And I care less what liberal-minded fools think about slavery. Slavery is an means to an end, this nation was founded on that, commerce and wealth dictate it.. It's been going on since the beginning of mankind, and will go on until the end, when our Lord Jesus parts the sky."

"You, sir," Robert said, "are a wanton, despicable human being."

The Colonel gave this some thought, walked back to Robert, and quickly brought his fist into contact with Robert's stomach. The impact made a horrible sound, and Robert fell to his knees, the wind knocked out of him. Then Robert started to vomit. Judas went to his friend, to help him up.

"I don't take kindly to critics," Colonel Charles K. Jodzio said, and to Judas: "You, boy, step away from him. Let him pick himself up."

Judas still tried to help Robert.

Jodzio took out a Colt six-shooter, cocked it, and aimed. "Boy, I said step away, *now.*"

Judas did as he was told.

"And what is your name, son?" Jodzio inquired.

"Payne."

"As in giving or receiving?" He chuckled, but his men didn't seem to know whether to join or not. "Cross me, and you will be receiving," he said, and asked: "What happened to your eye, kid?"

"I lost it when the wagon hit a rock," Judas said. "It just popped right out and bounced on the ground."

Jodzio chuckled, and this time his men, uncertain, joined. "Boy has a sense of humor," he said. " I can appreciate that." To Robert: "Get on your feet, Mister."

Robert stood up, wavering.

Jodzio slugged him in the stomach again, knocking Robert hard onto his back.

"ROBERT! NO!" Mary Jo Scroggins screamed from where the women were.

"And what do we have here?" Jodzio put his gun away, and walked over to the women. "Young lady, why are you so concerned about him?"

"Stop hurting him," Mary Jo said. "Leave him alone."

"And *why* do you care? Just good Christian ethic?"

"Because he's my husband!" she said, with defiance and strength.

"Is that so? And your name—?"

"Mary Jo Scroggins!"

"Ahhh. Well, Mr. Scroggins," turning back to Robert, who was now being helped up by several other men, but not Judas, "is this indeed your wife?"

"She is," Robert said, coughing.

"Not a bad looking young lady. I wonder what she looks like without those clothes. Does she have a nice body? I *won*der." He gestured to his men, and three of them grabbed Mary Jo. She tried to get away from them. Several men from the caravan started to make advances, and Jodzio's men pointed their guns. The three holding Mary Jo quickly, methodically, and laughing the whole time, proceeded to tear her dress and undergarments off until she was naked. Mary Jo tried to hide herself, but the assailants held her by both arms, as if she were being crucified, for the Colonel to inspect. He took his time looking her up and down, and reached out and squeezed one of her breasts. Mary Jo spat at him, but it flew past Jodzio's face. He smiled, and shook his head. He inspected her backside, a hand on his saber. "Not bad," he said, nodding. "I've seen better, but I've seen worse. Not bad. We'll have fun with her."

"You bastard!" Robert yelled.

"Yes," Jodzio replied, "I am." He raised his voice. "I believe you are all getting the picture of your future. The men will be working in the mines, and the women...will be working as concubines, keeping *me* and *my* men happy, and fed, and other various errands. Once in a while, I will allow—granted that there are no problems—conjugal visits for husbands and wives. Welcome to my world."

5.

With a gunman at each wagon, the caravan took a course North away from the trail. It was three days journey to Colonel Jodzio's silver mines. The sun was blaring down hot. No one spoke to each other—if they did, and Jodzio's men caught them, they were beaten. The women were kept from the men, and while nothing had happened yet, regarding the women and Jodzio's men, it was only a matter of time. Judas noticed the way Jodzio's men looked upon the women, and those expressions on their faces, the darkness in their eyes, made Judas feel sick.

Robert Kevin Scroggins remained silent during the whole journey, somber and contemplative. Judas wished he knew some way to console his friend; but the man had been humiliated, his own wife's nakedness exposed before everyone, his inability to do anything about it. Scroggins didn't need to say it, he didn't even need to show it on his face; Judas knew, and so did the others, that his manhood had been injured, and he wasn't unable to protect his spouse. Nut neither could any of the others, so Judas assumed no one held it against Scroggins.

They were all hungry. Jodzio's men didn't give them much of their own food, having it for themselves.

The night before they arrived, as they all huddled in one area to sleep, a blanket afforded to each, one young man said, softly,

"We have to do something."

"Yeah, of course we do," someone else said, "what?"

"We can't let them do this to us."

"They have guns."

Everyone mumbled. Judas looked at the night sky, so filled with stars...

"We will do something, eventually," Scroggins spoke up. Everyone hushed. "When the time is right. We have to wait. And when the time is right, we have to act quickly."

Whispers and nods of yes, of course, when the time is right.

The captor who was guarding them approached, rifle in hand. "What's all the talkin' about? What's so interestin'?"

No one answered.

"Stop talkin' and do some dreamin'," the guard said. "We arrive tomorrow. Y'all prolly work tomorrow. You need yer strength." He spat out some chewing tobacco, and went back to where he was standing before.

In another part of the camp, in one of the wagons, Colonel Charles K. Jodzio was enjoying himself with bottle of bourbon, a cigar, lounging about in his long johns that needed, he noted, a good washing. He'd have the women attend to laundry when they arrived at the mine. Speaking of women, he was waiting for one now. One of his men brought a lady with short dark hair and large eyes. He liked her eyes.

The woman stared at him, almost lifeless, with those eyes.

"What's your name, my dear?"

"Claire," she replied. "Claire Brooks."

"Would you care for a drink?" He held out the bottle.

"No thank you."

"It'll help make this easier," he said. "I had you brought to me first because you seemed to be the oldest of the women here."

"I'm twenty-nine," she said.

"Most of the other ladies seem quite young. And the men too. This is a good thing, in certain ways. Difficult in others. You're married, yes? How many years?"

"Three. I had a husband before that, but he died."

"I'm sorry."

"So am I. But I love my new husband very much."

"That's nice." Jodzio drank. "Do you know why you're here? What's expected of you?"

"I have an idea," she said flatly.

"After tonight, you will explain it to the other women."

"And if I refuse? Will you hurt me?"

"I will hurt your husband," Jodzio said. "I may even kill him, to make an example. I don't want to. I need all the strong labor I can get."

"You're an evil man."

"No. Just ambitious."

She stared at him, and said, "Let me have that bottle."

He smiled, and passed the bourbon over. Claire Brooks held it, looked at it. Jodzio had a pistol on her.

He said, "If you're thinking I'm drunk and you can hit me over the head with that bottle, remove such fantasies from your pretty head at once."

She raised the bottle to her mouth and took a long drink.

"My my," the Colonel said. "You like your booze."

She coughed. "No. I don't. But you're right, sir—it will help make the horrible thing I am about to go through easier."

"Horrible? Must you insult me?"

"Horrible," she said, and drank, and coughed.

"You may even enjoy it," he said.

"That I will not," she said. "You may do what dirty deed you will do, but I will not enjoy it, and I will not call it making love."

"I never call it making love," Jodzio said. "I just call it screwin'."

She took another drink, and handed the bottle back.

"Take your clothes off," Jodzio said, "and lie here on this blanket."

"Will you turn the lamp off?" she asked.

"I will turn it down, but not off." He lowered the oil lamp some.

There were tears in the woman's eyes.

"Don't be sad," he told her.

"I don't want to do this," she said.

"I understand. But you have to."

"And I imagine I will be doing it often, with your men."

"It may seem brutal and immoral at first, but you, and the others, will learn to accept it."

"You talk as if you have done this before."

"Oh, I have," Jodzio said, "there are other women at the mine. Now enough with talk, undress and lie down."

Claire Brooks took her time taking her skirt, blouse, and undergarments off, but the bourbon was already hitting her and making her dizzy. She laid down and closed her eyes.

Jodzio started to get out of his long johns. "You're easier than normal," he said. "It's curious. You act like *you* have done this before. And not just with your husbands."

"I was no virgin before my first marriage," she said, very softly, looking away, eyes still closed. The alcohol was burning in her blood, and she remembered another life, a life long ago, "I worked some saloons when I was a girl. It's something my husband doesn't know, an never will know, just like he will never know of this moment or any other."

He was hovering over her. "Well, well."

She opened her eyes. "Just do it and get it over with so I can go."

"You don't understand, Claire Brooks." He got on top of her. "You're staying with me all night. And we're going to have an interesting time all night."

6.

Her name was Doña Maldita; she was forty-eight years old, thin as a scarecrow with dark, wrinkled skin, but held herself with a certain amount of elegance and power, as a woman in her profession needed to. She was in a small, dirty backroom watching a young blonde girl being humped by a man badly in need of a shave—all over his body. The man was repulsive, and he was one of the saloon owners. The girl was doing a fair job acting like she enjoyed it, moaning and moving her hips back and forth. The hairy man spent himself, then sat up and buttoned his trousers. He was smiling. The girl lay there, legs spread, staring at the ceiling.

"What do you think?" the man said. "She's one of my best, too. I'll miss her if you take her off my hands."

Doña Maldita stood, and grabbed a blanket to cover the girl. "When they are done," she said, "you will close your legs and cover yourself. Only a cheap whore lies there spilling seed waiting for the next customer."

"But she is a cheap whore," the man laughed.

"Not after she works for me."

"So you wanna buy her?"

"Yes," the woman said. To the girl: "Clean yourself when we leave."

Doña Maldita hated scouting small towns for whores. But she needed more girls, her enterprises in Texas were expanding. She returned to the front of the saloon, where her two bodyguards waited, quick and swift young thugs whom she knew since they were children.

"So, that's three whores you're buying," the hairy man said, pouring himself a whiskey. "Why not buy them all?"

"Because the other three don't know how to fuck," Doña Maldita said. "Now let's talk prices so I can leave this hellhole."

After purchasing the whores, and gathering the girls and their belongings to join her in the hotel she was staying at, Doña Maldita felt like drawing a long hot bath. Instead, she lay on the bed and took a short nap. What the hell was the name of this town? Hand. Hand, Kansas, just outside Fort Larned. How had she gotten here? Someone had told her there was a saloon in Hand that wasn't doing much business, or one of the owners had mismanaged the profits, or something, and the whores there were for sale.

A few more girls to ship off to Dallas, and she'd return home.

She woke up, one of her young bodyguards standing by her

bed. She thought, at first, the boy wanted to lay with her, as she sometimes did with these strong beautiful boys, but there wasn't any lust in his eyes.

"What is it, *mijo*?"

"There is a man downstairs, he wishes an audience with you," said the bodyguard.

"Am I expecting this man?"

"No. He says he has business."

"Who is this man?"

"He would not give me his name." The boy looked troubled for a moment. "He is a man of God, Doña."

"What do you say?" She was on her feet. Her bones cracked. She did not like getting old. She would like—she thought—a quick roll on the bed with the boy; that always made her feel vibrant and alive, to know she still had the sex drive in her.

Sex, however, for Doña Maldita, was more often an ugly thing, and a means to make her wealthy.

The bodyguard said, "He wears the black and white outfit of the Anglo's church. And a hat. But he looks like a magician or a trickster." He added, "And he is missing an arm."

This piqued her curiosity. "Give me ten minutes," she said, "and then show him in."

The bodyguard nodded, and left.

Hurriedly, Maldita fixed her hair and touched up her make-up, smoothed out of her skirt and glanced at herself in the mirror. She never saw the woman she was today in that reflection; she saw the raging beauty that she was when she was fifteen, the whore everyone in Mexico wanted when she was twenty.

A man of God with one arm? The thought gave her chills. Could this, she wondered, have any connection to the images that haunted her dreams since she was a child? Always the shadowy men with some part of their body missing: a leg, an arm, an eye, an ear, a foot, even parts of their heads. When she was small, these men were fatherly, and she wasn't afraid; as she got older, the men would chase her, hurt her, sometimes brutally make love to her. They still haunted her dreams from time to time.

Considering this, she almost summoned the boy back to tell the Anglo to go away, that she would not be granting anyone an audience.. But she felt, she knew, that whoever this man was, he'd just come back, and probably find her before she could collect her whores and go south.

A knock on her door, the bodyguard entered. "He is here, Doña."

"Thank you, niño."

The bodyguard retreated, and the tall, gaunt, pale man in a black jacket and trousers, white collar, and one arm, entered. He removed his hat with his good arm.

"Good day, ma'am."

She smiled. "Is it a good day, sir?"

"I beg your pardon?"

"Why do you wish to see me, sir? I was told it was business."

"It is business."

"If you're here to try and save my soul," she said, "do not waste your time. My soul was forsaken long ago."

"I realize this," the man said. "You walk with the devil, as many do in these trying days."

Maldita had a horrible thought—maybe he wasn't a preacher, maybe it was a costume, and he was an assassin. She had her share of enemies who would gladly se her dead. But she also knew her boys checked him for weapons before allowing him to pass. Still—although he had only one arm, his hand looked strong, strong enough to choke her, to break her neck.

I am becoming paranoid in my years, she thought.

"You do know what business I am in?" she asked.

"Yes," he said, "I do."

She laughed. "So what does a preacher want with a Madame? Do you wish to sample the sins of the flesh with one of my young girls? Do you have a circle of deacons who would like a private and secret party of naked young women?"

The man considered this, frowning. "I hope that you jest."

"Thinking out loud."

"These things do not actually happen."

"I have long overcome the shock of what pious and virtuous men do to women behind closed doors," she assured him.

"I am Reverend Jedediah Payne," he said.

"That is good for you," she replied, not giving her name. She assumed he knew her name, if he knew her business.

"My church is in Tyburn, a town about twenty miles east of here. A member of my flock, a sincere elderly woman, had heard rumor that a Madame from lower Texas was in the vicinity purchasing whores for her houses of ill repute. Naturally, my first inclination was to seek you out and, yes, try to save your soul, or at best drive you away from our influence. In fact, I would like you to leave Kansas immediately, but I am in a position to make a business transaction. I have a young harlot I wish to sell to you."

"A man of God? Selling me a whore?" She laughed at this.

"It sounds absurd, but the circumstances—"

"And *what* whore do you know, Reverend?"

"She is not a practicing whore, but it is in her blood, and I am sure she will be more suited to life with you, than corrupting my home."

"And what right do you have to sell her?" Maldita asked. "Surely, a man of your nature does not *own* a whore."

"She is my daughter," he said.

7.

Each morning and night, Robert Kevin Scroggins held prayer among the captive men working the silver mines belonging to Colonel Jodzio and his highwaymen. The enslaved men consisted not only those who were part of the caravan, but a dozen others who had been captured in a previous caravan two months before. At first, Judas Payne joined, or pretended to join, closing his eyes and lowering his head, all the while thinking about the hard work, which was more difficult than the work he had to do on his father's land.

There were about forty men, from Judas' initial count, all housed under one large canvas tent and guarded, at the entrance, by two armed "Jodzioites" (as someone coined the term, humorous at first, but now having the ring of distaste). On the other side of the small mountain, which was being mined, were two other large tents: one for women, one for the rest of Jodzio's men. No one talked about what was going on over there. No one wanted to know, even if they did know.

They received three meals a day—breakfast, lunch, and dinner, which was often the same thing: grits and beans and stale bread and dirty water. Jodzio was fond of saying that while it was not the best grub around, it was enough to sustain them, and "better than what most niggers and Chinese slaves get."

Of which, there were several Negro and Chinese mine workers, who were, ironically enough, in foreman positions, telling them what to do in the mines. They were housed in a smaller tent nearby, which was left unguarded.

They went to work at six a.m. sharp, entering the main entrance of the small mountain, split into groups for various tunnels. Each group was guarded by a single armed man. At eleven, they had a half hour lunch break, and they worked until five or six, at which time they had dinner (all meals, they were reminded, prepared by their own wives). Then they retired to their communal tent, where most collapsed from exhaustion.

One day, Scroggins said to Judas, "The Jodzioites didn't tunnel this mountain out. None of them did a hard day's work here, ever. I don't even think Jodzio prospected and made claim. He stole the property. I bet he even killed the original owner."

It was back-breaking, trying, and heart-breaking work. The men dug and tunneled, sifted through rock, hauled silver out by the barrel-full. Judas could understand the worth of such work if this were your land, your silver to become rich from; or if you were being paid well. But this was forced labor, with no end to it in site, it was always uncomfortably hot both inside and outside the mountain, and at the best all they could expect was the measly morsels of food, a blanket on the floor, and the incessant worry for their wives and children on the other side.

While work may have kept their minds off what their wives were going through, each day Judas could see it growing on their faces: weariness and the desire to give up, coupled with fear and worry, but the acceptance of that fear and worry. While a lot of the men—Scroggins included—were, at the beginning, defiant and ready to fight for their freedom at any opportune moment, that fire soon dwindled as the days became weeks.

Scroggins held his ground, and often tried to boost morale. "Jodzio knows that working us to weakness is the best way to defeat any acts of rebellion. We must find the strength to stand against the Jodzioites, not only in our hearts, but in our faith in God."

Someone said, "God? There is God here. God has looked away from us."

Someone else said, "Perhaps it was a sin to leave home and look for a new life and we are being punished."

"No, *no,* NO," Scroggins cried, frustrated at the defeatism. "Life is a big test, filled with many smaller tests. This is but another test."

"Then God is a hard teacher," Judas heard himself say. He was surprised by the words that came from his mouth. As quickly as they came out, he wished he could retract them.

Scroggins considered Judas for a moment, then nodded. "Yes," he said, "this is true. God is a hard teacher, and he wants us all to pass his tests with good grades."

"Bullshit," someone said.

And someone else: "Go to sleep, Scroggins. It'll be morning sooner than you think."

One young fellow from the caravan, Billy Patricks, always listened to Scroggins—he looked up to the man for strength and wisdom, and wasn't about to give up. He had a lot of fight. "There are only two guards posted outside each night," he said, "and forty of us."

Someone said: "And each guard has two pistols and a rifle."

"Some may die," Patricks said, "but it's a sacrifice that has to be made, for the overall good. We will be free, and then we can rescue the women and children."

Someone: "How do we know that there's just two? It could be a ploy. There may be two others out in the darkness."

"There are only fifteen Jodzioites in all," Patricks said. "They're not everywhere."

Someone: "How do we know the niggers and chinks don't have guns? They seem well enough in cahoots with the Jodzioites."

Someone: "Yeah, I think the niggers and chinks are with them and could be armed as well."

"I doubt that," Scroggins spoke up. "I admire your determination, Billy. But say we do overtake the guards. That gives us what? Four pistols and two rifles among forty men? Less those that may die in the overtaking? Then we have to go to the other camp and fight the Jodzioites and all their weapons. And those men, need I remind you, are hardened veterans of the War. They are soldiers who are experts in guns and hand-to-hand combat. Who among us has fought in battle?"

All the young men looked down, and no one raised their hand.

Then they went to sleep.

A few days later, in the tunnels, Billy Patricks went about telling everyone his plan. He would, tonight, fake sickness—grave illness. "I'll act as if I have the cholera," he said, "I've seen people who had it, I know how they act, how they wither in pain and despair. We will tell the guards that I need immediate medical attention. When the guards come in to look upon me screaming in pain, in all the commotion, we will jump them, kill them, take their guns, and make ourselves free."

It was a wild idea but Patricks enlisted the help of enough of the men, including Scroggins.

"It's worth a try," Scroggins admitted. "At this point, anything is."

So that evening, as planned, Patricks fell to the ground, crying, clutching his gut, withering about in the dirt like a man possessed by something foul. Judas thought he was doing a good performance. Others called out to the guards for help. Both guards came in, rifle in one hand, pistol in the other.

Shouts and pleas: "He's sick! He has the cholera! He needs a doctor now! He needs to be taken out of here!"

The guards went to inspect Patrick, who was still moaning and twitching.

One of the guards said, "What ails him, you say?"

"It must be the cholera!" someone said. "I've seen it before."

The two guards looked at each other. They nodded, in unison, and one shot Patricks twice in the chest with his pistol.

A silence fell throughout the tent, as well as a collective wave of shock and surprise.

"Can't have the cholera spreading around this camp," the guard who'd fired said. "Okay, I need two men to cart this body out."

The two men were Scroggins and Judas.

The next day, another man was killed. Colonel Jodzio, for the first time since the capture of the caravan, gathered everyone at the foot of the mountain, men and women separated as usual. The children were not present. Wives cried out to their husbands, husbands to their wives, until the Jodzioites silenced them with stares, pointed guns, and fists.

Jodzio, in full military regalia and his saber, hat on head, medals shining in the sun, stood between the two groups and spoke loudly.

"It is time for a lesson," he said. He nodded to one of his men, who brought out a young lady from the women's side. She was bruised and blood was dried around her lips.

"Helen," one of the enslaved men said.

Jodzio paced and he spoke. "It was explained, and expected, that each woman would have her share of work to do: preparing food, doing laundry, and keeping me and my men very happy."

The Jodzioites all laughed.

"This young lady here has been resistant. You see," turning to the men, "I first sample each young lady. I determine how good she is in the sack, and if there's any special talents she may have that my men will enjoy. But this strong-willed girl has been refusing to do one of her duties. She cooks, yes, and she can launder clothes, yes, *but she will not screw.* I cannot have such defiance here, it doesn't suit well with my program. So it is necessary to break her will. Who among you here is this fine young lady's husband?"

The fellow who'd called her name raised his hand and said proudly, "I am!"

"Bring him here," Jodzio said to one of his men.

"No," Scroggins said, but it was a whisper. "No..."

The young man was brought forward, feet away from his wife. Both were made to kneel and face each other. The young woman, Helen, was crying, and so was her husband.

"Helen?" Jodzio said.

She cried.

"Helen," the Colonel said, "do you love him?"

"I love him more than anything," she wept, "and he is the only man who will ever know me!"

Jodzio pulled out his saber and drove it straight through the young man's chest, the blade, covered in blood, exiting out his back.

Helen screamed, tried to go to her husband; she was restrained by one of the Jodzioites. The other women cried out in shared agony and fear, perhaps terrified that the same would happen to their husbands. Of the men, there was only silence.

Jodzio pulled his saber free, and the young man fell forward, dead, his face almost landing in the lap of his hysterical wife.

Jodzio took out a cloth from his back pocket and cleaned his sword. "Now Helen doesn't have to worry about her virtue," he said, more to the women than anyone else. "She's a widow. And for any other woman who does not do what is expected of her, she too will become a widow." He raised his voice, to speak to all. "This is not something I want to do. I have lost two workers already, and they are workers much needed. You are all needed. All I ask is that you do what is expected of you, do as you're told, and no more death will occur. The man from last night, he did not have the cholera." To the men's side: "I don't know what you had planned, but I can surmise what it may have been. My advice: Do Not Try Anything Foolish."

It was more like a motto to live by in the weeks and months to follow.

8.

Evangeline Payne didn't know her father was out of town. She figured he was at his church. Sheriff Lish knew the Reverend had gone to Hand for some sort of business that was neither the Sheriff's concern nor care. The Reverend's lack of presence was a good excuse to ride out to the Payne's and pay another visit to the girl he felt he could marry.

Evangeline wasn't all that surprised to have the Sheriff call on her. She had hoped he would soon. She knew what was on his mind, given that kiss between them.

"I just wanted to see how you're doing, Miss Payne," he said.

"Very fine, thank you," she lied. "And you can call me Evangeline, if you like."

"I would rather call you 'angel,'" he said.

The word sent terror and cold through her blood and body. "Angel" is what she called her one and only love, her dearest, whom she did her best to keep out of her mind so as not to go insane. She started to say something, but she didn't know what to say.

"Has anyone ever called you 'Angel'?" Lish asked. "It's a fitting na—"

"Stop, no," she held up a hand. "I *do not* wish to be called that."

"I'm sorry. Evangeline?"

She would not cry in front of this man, not now, not ever. She would only cry in private. If she showed him tears, showed him her weakness, he would want to know why, and she might tell him.

She said, "Perhaps, for now, you should refer to me in the proper, as Miss Payne, for we hardly know much of each other, now do we, Sheriff?"

"No," he said, fumbling around with his hat. "Perhaps it was a mistake having come out here. Maybe..."

He started to back away. Evangeline said, "Don't be foolish, Sheriff Lish. Come on inside and rest a bit. I know the ride out here is always trying on the body."

Not the body, Lish wanted to say.

They sat across from each other at the table. Sunlight shone through the window and glared off the old wood. Neither of them knew what to say to the other.

"Would you care for some lunch?" Evangeline asked. "I can make sandwiches with jam. We may have some peanut butter as well. And I know we have some oatmeal cookies."

"Well," Lish said. He smiled. "Yes. Yes, some lunch would be nice."

Evangeline stood, pleased that she at least had a task to do. "I shan't take long."

"Would you care for some help?" He almost stood up, but ceased when she held out her hand, the same way she had when she didn't want him to call her *angel.* "I..."

"No help is needed, Mr. Lish," she said. "This is my chore and my chore alone, and you will be pleased with the result, I hope. I'm rather talented in the kitchen. Not having had a mother, I have been cooking for my father and—" She almost said brother. She had to watch herself. "For my father and guests since I was a child this high," indicating, with her hand flat, a level at her mid-section.

"I'll wait then," Lish said.

Smiling, Evangeline retreated to the kitchen. Her heart was pumping fast. Why was she entertaining this man? Oh, but she knew why. Stop questioning yourself!

She returned, fifteen minutes later, with the sandwiches and cookies, as well as lemonade.

They sat quietly at the table and ate.

Finally, Evangeline broke the silence. "Is your job very dangerous?"

"Not usually, no."

"You carry a gun."

"All men carry guns these days," Lish laughed, placing a napkin at his mouth.

"Have you had to use your gun?"

"Once or twice."

"Have you ever killed men?"

"No, not as a Sheriff," he said.

"But you have killed men?"

"In the War."

She nodded. "Men kill men in wars. It is the nature of war, is it not?"

"Yes, I'm afraid so."

"But you never have to deal with hooligans and rough necks?"

"Not usually. Tyburn is a bit out of the way. Sure one day I'll have to, I reckon. And maybe I'll have to hire a deputy or two to help."

"Yes, that's right. You are alone in your job."

I'm alone, he wanted to say. "You ask a lot of questions, Miss Payne."

"Please, may call me Evangeline. I'm afraid I was being a bit brash and testy a while back."

"Evangeline. I like saying your name."

She laughed, lightly, and—demurely—looked away.

He said, "Did I say something funny?"

"No, not at all," the girl said. "It just occurred to me that I don't know your name. I have been calling you Sheriff and Mister."

"Paul," he said.

"Paul," she said. "Paul," she said again.

"Evangeline." He *loved* saying her name.

When it was time for him to go, Evangeline saw him to the door. He was just going to leave, but he mustered the courage to say, "May I kiss you again, before I head back to town?"

"No," she said. "Not yet. Last time was a fluke, an accident by all means. I am not a girl who rushes into romance."

Lish felt his knees shake. "Is this romance?"

"I do not know," she said. "What do you think? Have you ever been in love, Paul?"

"I don't think so," he told her. "I think—I thought, at certain times, in my life, that I was. But now I'm not sure. Have you?"

"Have I?"

"Been in love?"

"I'm just a girl out here alone on my father's land. What do I know of love?" And she lied again: "No, Sheriff Paul Lish, I do not know love. I wonder if I will know it when it comes."

"You will."

"Then I have hope," she said softly.

"I sure would love to kiss you again."

"A kiss would be nice," she said, "but not today."

"May I ask—?"

"Yes?"

"Would you truly possible, ever," he was choking on his words, "would it be possible for an old fellow like me to attract the interest a girl so young and attractive as yourself?"

"Yes," she heard herself say.

"Even for marriage?"

"You certainly rush into things," she said. "One thing at a time, one day at a time. Marriage is something a girl needs to think about quite seriously."

"Of course...."

"But anything is possible," she said.

She watched him ride away. She would never love him, but she would marry him, to get away from her father once and for all.

A few hours after the Sheriff had departed, the Reverend came home. Evangeline fled to her room. She didn't expect him to come to her door.

"Open up, girl," he said.

"No," she said.

"We have a visitor. I would like you to pay your respects."

"What visitor?"

"A woman from out of town. Do not be rude. Open the door and say hello to her."

She hesitated, but opened her door. The sight of her one-armed father was ghastly. "Where is this woman?" she asked, expecting a trick.

"Waiting to see you," the Reverend said.

The woman in question was sitting in the exact spot at the table where the Sheriff had sat. Evangeline thought she looked like an old witch. Her skin was brown like her beloved's.

"My dear, my dear," the woman said, standing, smiling with a mouthful of very white teeth. "Aren't *you* a lovely one? And what did your father say your name was?"

"Evangeline," the Reverend said.

"Oh yes. What a beautiful name." The older woman held out her thin, long red-nailed hand to the younger woman. "I am Maldita."

Reluctantly, Evangeline took the woman's hand, which was cold and bony.

"Let us all sit down and talk," Maldita suggested.

"Let us sit down," the Reverend said, "yes."

And talk about what? Evangeline wanted to say.

"But first, but first!" Maldita was cheerful, turning to a bag next to her. "I have here," and she brought out a small bottle, "the absolutely finest apple cider from Mexico. You have never tasted a cider so wonderful. My dear Evangeline," she said, "would you be kind enough to fetch three glasses, so we can share this cider and talk?"

"Yes," the Reverend said, "three glasses."

Evangeline went to the kitchen.

Cautiously, quietly, Maldita whispered, "Do not drink a sip of the cider."

The Reverend opened his mouth, and the Madame stopped him with a shake of her head.

"You didn't tell she was so beautiful," Maldita said.

"Yes," the Reverend said, "I did."

"Perhaps I did not believe you."

Evangeline returned with three glasses. Maldita poured the cider in each glass.

Evangeline looked at liquid. It had an enticing aroma.

"Taste it, dear," Maldita said. "I value your opinion."

Evangeline brought the glass to her lips. She stopped, to smell it again. Maldita was smiling, her father had his usual ominous expression. She took a sip. The cider was warm, but sweet and delicious, sending a tingle up her spine and to her head.

"This is wonderful," she said.

"It is the finest in all the land," Maldita said. "Drink up. There is plenty of more."

Evangeline drank half the glass, savoring the taste on her tongue.

"Tell me, my dear," the older woman said, "what is it that you enjoy the most? What are your interests?"

She was feeling light and dizzy all of the sudden.

"Well, I love to read books," she blurted, then fell face down on the table, unconscious.

"I hope she did not bruise that pretty nose," Doña Maldita said, pursing her lips.

"There was something in the cider," Reverend Payne said.

"Of course."

"Was that necessary?"

"You do not believe that she would come with me willingly and of her own free will, do you?"

"No," he said.

"And what do you care? You want to be rid of her, am I correct?"

"Yes."

"She is *absolutely* gorgeous. I will make a *lot* of money off her over the years."

"Do what you must," Payne said softly.

"And she is not a virgin?"

"She is a whore," he said. "She will undoubtedly enjoy

anything you toss her way."

"Good," Maldita said. "Call my boys inside, and we will take her. Oh, I suppose we must talk a price here. I am sure you want a good deal of money for her, yes?"

"Whatever you think she's worth."

"What is she worth to you?"

"Not a dime."

"I will pay you more than a dime," Maldita laughed.

What she did pay the Reverend, he was not expecting. When she and her two bodyguards had left with the unconscious Evangeline, along with a few clothes Maldita took from the girl's bedroom, Reverend Jedediah Payne sat up for a long time, in the dark house, looking a the wad of American bills on the table. Such a sum would go far at the church, but there might be questions. Later, he burned every bill to a cinder.

9.

Every day, from morning until night, Mary Jo Scroggins cooked up schemes in her mind on how she would escape her captors. She had daydreams; in each, Colonel Jodzio died, sometimes at her own hands, sometimes by the hands of her husband. She knew Robert was having the same thoughts; they were like-minds, meant for each other, perhaps soul mates. They would both see this ordeal through, they would come out of this alive and wiser, and be together once again. She would get her life back, the way it was meant to be, one way or the other....

Mending and washing dirty pants and shirts, re-soling boots, cooking food, these chores weren't that hard. What was hard on the women here was the sexual favors they had to give up for the Jodzioites. The girl, Helen, whose husband had been murdered before all their eyes, had lost the fight in her, and had finally given herself over to Jodzio. The next night, several men came in, and they took her away, drinking and laughing. Sometimes the men would come straight into the tent and rape whatever woman he pleased, in front of all. Mary Jo would look away, pushing out the sounds of the woman's cries, the man's grunts. What horrible savages these men were, to do such an act out in the open. Most of the time, however, when a Jodzioite came in, and picked a woman he wanted, he would take her away. It was worse when there were several of them that took one woman, Mary Jo couldn't even imagine the horror. But the worse—yes, the most vile—were the women who'd been here before her arrival, five of them, who seemed to enjoy their trysts with the Jodzioites. They would joke about who was their favorite, who lasted longer, who kissed well.

One time, Mary Jo said to one of these women, "How can you let yourself find pleasure with them?"

The woman was serious when she said, "What else can I do? I've been here for months. I don't like being afraid. If you don't fight them, they aren't rough with you. Sometimes they can be nice."

"What about your husband?" Mary Jo asked.

"He died when Jodzio captured us. I will mourn for him properly when I'm free. But I'm here, and I have to make the best of it. Do you think I'd choose between having fun and running away? I would run in a second if I could. But I won't live every day here moping around and crying out to God about misfortune."

Another of the veteran women said to her: "My husband is on the other side, but I haven't been near him once. It's good to have a man's attention, even it is with these roughnecks. I'm not proud of myself. But I'm making the best of this situation. I've long gotten over the shock."

Mary Jo just didn't understand.

A woman who was with their caravan, Claire Brooks, took Mary Jo aside by her arm. "Don't trouble them with such talk," Claire Brooks said. "They may seem like they're having fun on the outside, but they are in torment inside. I have seen such look on women. If pretending to enjoy themselves with the Jodzioites helps them get through each day, let them have that."

"It is so *disgusting.*"

"You don't even know yet."

"No," Mary Jo said, "I don't."

Thus far, she had been spared having to be violated any Jodzioites; Jodzio himself had not yet had her in his tent. There was only one other woman who was spared as well, then one night she was taken to Jodzio, and the next day she was hauled away, at different hours, by most of the Jodzioites. For days, the girl walked around in a daze.

The following night, Mary Jo Scroggins was summoned by Jodzio. She pushed all fear deep into her core, and told herself that she knew this day would come. She realized she hadn't properly prepared herself, because she didn't know how.

Jodzio was bare-chested, his long johns pulled down to his waist, drinking a bottle of whiskey. He was a hairless, muscular man with a long scar down his belly, and small, circular scars at his shoulders that she thought were bullet wounds.

"Ah, Mrs. Scroggins," he said. "At last. Would you care for some whiskey?"

"I do not drink," she told him.

"It will help.

"Be done with it. I don't need your small talk."

He laughed.

She said, "And I suppose if I refused to give you my favors, you would threaten to kill my husband."

"I wouldn't threaten," the Colonel said. "I'd do it."

She knew he was not bluffing.

"Your husband is an interesting man, as are you. Please sit down with me here. Not please. I insist. It's an order."

She sat down, but kept her distance.

Jodzio drank and talked. "I chose you to be the last woman for a reason. Believe it or not, I pay close attention to each and every member of this camp. If I don't do it myself, my men give me reports. You are much like your husband. I imagine that is why you both married."

"My husband is a very good man," she said.

"I'm sure he is. He seems a strong-willed man, and he seems like the leader. He is always offering words of wisdom and advice to the men, leading them in prayer, boosting morale."

"He is a natural at that."

"Yes. I believe you are as well. Are you the leader of the women's tent?"

"We have no 'leader,' Colonel Jodzio."

"But you could be the leader."

"I don't understand."

"The women need someone to speak for them, to keep the order, should order fall. I like you, Mrs. Scroggins. I like you very much, since the first day. In another life, had we met, when I was a fine young officer, I may have courted you, and taken you for my own wife, and we could have had children."

"I seriously doubt that."

"I have a proposition for you. You take a leadership role among the women, you report to me how they feel, what they're unhappy about, what they would like to change. You will be, say, my liaison. In return, you will not have to give yourself to any man in this camp but me."

She didn't know what to say.

She didn't have to say anything. She didn't have a choice.

When Jodzio had her three times that night, she kept her eyes closed. She didn't sleep when he did, snoring loudly next to her.

In the morning, Jodzio summoned Judas Payne to his tent. He was shaving, fighting off the effects of the whiskey, and remembering the pleasures of Mary Jo Scroggins' body.

"You're probably wondering why I called you here, boy," Jodzio said.

"No."

"No? Of course you are. Payne, is it? Your name is Payne?"

"Yes."

"What are you, Mr. Payne?"

"Pardon me?"

"You're not white. Not all white. Your skin, your features..."

"I'm nothing," Judas said.

"Are you part Mex? Part Indian?"

"I don't know, sir."

"You don't know?"

"No, sir."

"What race was your mother?"

"I don't know."

"How could a man not know what race his mother was?"

"She died when I was a child. I never knew her."

"I see," Jodzio said. "And your father?"

"He also died."

"Did they die together?"

"I don't know."

"And I suppose you don't know what race your father was?"

"No," Judas lied.

"Well, you're something. How did you lose that eye?"

"In a fight."

"With who?"

"I don't remember."

Jodzio laughed. "You would've made a fine soldier in my regiment, Mr. Payne. Captured by the South, you would've given them a run during an interrogation. I have an offer to make you, Mr. Payne."

"Sir?"

"Are you interested?

"I don't know."

"I have the niggers and chinks acting as foremen for a reason," Jodzio said. "Do you know what this reason is?"

"No, sir."

"Because all their lives they have been pushed around by white men. As lackeys, underpaid laborers, and slaves. Now this is their chance to get even. That is why I can trust them. They enjoy their position, and where else would they go? I need another foreman. I thought that you, being a man of color and questionable breed, and possibly having lead a life under the harsh rule of white men, would enjoy a turn of the table. You would get to sleep in a different tent, without guard, and get more food. And you wouldn't have to work so hard."

"I think you may have misjudged me, sir," Judas Payne said.

"Perhaps. But think it over."

10.

Evangeline Payne woke up to movement. Her hands and feet were bound by rope. She was in the back of some covered wagon. Was this a dream? The last thing she recalled was drinking wonderful apple cider with her father and the dark-skinned woman—

That very woman, in different clothes, clothes more suitable for road travel, was sitting next to her.

"Good morning, dear," the woman said.

Evangeline, dumbfounded, didn't know what to say.

"Before you ask a dozen questions," Doña Maldita said, "let me explain everything to you. There was a drug in the cider. Your father sold you to me. We are going to Texas, where you will be in my—employ—until you reach your thirtieth birthday. At that time, I will give you the collected sum of the shares of the money you earned, and you may leave if you choose. Or you could choose to stay. But old whores don't do as much business as young whores. But if you still have your looks when you're thirty—"

Evangeline screamed.

11.

Mary Jo Scroggins wasn't exactly sure what was expected of her, but Jodzio had kept his word, and no other man touched her except him. Fortunately, he only had her brought to him once or twice a week. If any of the other women noticed that she was receiving special treatment, they didn't say. Mary Jo knew no one was paying much attention to anyone but themselves and their own circumstance and requirements. Occasionally, Jodzio asked her what the overall feelings of the women were, what they talked about. She said: "They're worried about their husbands, and they talk about their husbands," which was generally true.

"Are you worried about your husband?" he asked her. They were lying on the floor, on blankets, naked. It was a warm night. Her arms covered her breasts. He was touching her hair, her face, her stomach and legs...she did not allow herself to feel his touch.

"That is an absurd thing to ask me," Mary Jo Scroggins said. "Of course I am."

"He's a lucky man."

"Please," she said. "I don't want to talk about him."

"Of course. But I wanted to tell you that tomorrow...I will allow him to visit you. I will give you two hours together."

"I don't understand."

"What's to understand? You would like two hours with him, would you not?"

"Yes," she said.

"We'll make it three hours," Jodzio said. "This is my gift to you."

She didn't allow herself hope. Jodzio could have been playing a horrible trick on her, a ruse for his own sick amusement. Late the following day, he continued to prove to be a man of his word. She was taken to a different small tent later and there was Robert. He was dirty from work, and thinner for lack of proper food, but he looked well. They hugged each other and cried. They kissed one another and professed their love and devotion. They prayed to God, and held each other closely.

"Is it bad in the mine?" she asked him.

"It's hard work," he said. "You get used to it."

"Robert, *don't* get used to it. *Never* get used to it."

"I won't," he said, unable to look in her eyes.

"When will this end?"

"Trust in God," Robert said.

"I try. Faith is..."

"It's as if faith has died," he said. "Mine has not."

"No," she said, "no."

"Mary Jo," he said later. "I must ask you something. I must. I have to know. It tears at my heart. The knowledge of it may kill me, but I have to know."

She knew what he was going to ask. She couldn't look at him. Maybe he would change his mind.

"Have you been defiled?"

"No," she said, and was surprised how easily the lie came.

"Mary Jo?"

"Some have, and are," she said, "but not every woman. I have been spared."

"Oh thank God!" He embraced her.

I am a lair, she thought. But how could she tell him? She knew him well enough to know that it would certainly destroy him....

The three hours went by quickly, and Robert was taken from her. She wondered when she'd see him again. Every moment of those three hours would keep her going, keep her strong. She would savor the memory of every kiss, every tear, every touch.

She was taken to Jodzio next.

"Thank you," she said, "for what you did."

The Colonel smiled. "I'm not such a horrible beast, am I?"

"Will you let the other women see their husbands?"

"Yes," he said. "One woman, one a day, will get a visit."

"It will help them," she said.

He moved close to her, and kissed her on the lips.

"Kiss me like I'm your lover," he said.

She opened her mouth, but there was no emotion.

"Tell me, and tell me true," Jodzio said. "Did Robert make love to you today?"

"That is none of your concern," she said.

"Everything here is my concern. There is no privacy. I want to know. Did you make love to your husband?"

"No," she said.

"I don't believe that. You haven't been with him in two months—"

"Colonel Jodzio—"

"Call me Charles. You can now."

"Colonel Jodzio," she said, "unlike you, sexual intercourse is not on every man's mind. My marriage is based on the heart and soul." She would not tell him that they had tried to make love, but Robert was unable to perform, and was ashamed because of it.

"How pretty," Jodzio laughed. "Well, since your husband didn't make love to you, I will."

12.

Evangeline Payne kept her eyes closed as she stood naked in the middle of a bedroom, Doña Maldita circling about her, poking and touching. "Such fine smooth skin, and so pale," the woman said. "And not a wrinkle or a blemish. Not a scar, not a mole. You are like an artist's painting, my dear. You are nearly perfect. I envy you. I wonder at my luck. You will bring in much money. You will be very popular. And you will be very tired from fucking all day and night," she laughed. "You *do* know how to fuck, yes?"

Evangeline knew she was in Texas somewhere, but she didn't know where. She'd been kept locked in this room; she knew this was a house of prostitution. She could hear the music and laughter downstairs, the sounds of coupling from other rooms.

"Well?" Maldita said. "Do you or don't you?"

"I have never been with a man."

"Nonsense. Your father told me you were a *tramp.*"

"Pardon me?"

"That you had boys in your room left and right, strangers who passed by..."

"My father is a liar!"

Maldita frowned. "You are telling me you are a virgin, child?"

"Yes!"

"It is you who lie!"

"I am not like you or the other women here!"

"I shall see if this is true." With her fingers, Maldita made an inspection. She was surprised. "You are a virgin."

Evangeline was trembling. "I told you..."

"Why would your father lie? Why would he sell you to me?"

"He is a *mad man.* He is not what he seems." She took in a breath. "Will you let me go now?" she asked, hopefully.

Maldita raised her eyebrows. "Young girl, I do not know why your father did what he did, I do not know if he is a man of God as he said. Whatever his reasons do not matter anymore. I paid good money for you. You belong to me. You are my property. I have great plans for you."

"I am a virgin, not a whore!" Evangeline protested. "I am pure," she wept.

"Exactly," Maldita said, "and some wealthy gentleman will pay a handsome price for the honor of deflowering you."

13.

The following is a rather sad affair concerning the captivity of the men and women at Colonel Jodzio's silver mine. It is one that Judas Payne knew of, and observed, the memory of which (among other memories) would haunt him for all his days.

Among the men, there was a twenty-year-old fellow by the name of Maurice Blevins. He had an eighteen-year-old wife, Tammy Blevins, whom he'd known and loved since she was fourteen and he was sixteen, in more innocent days in a small Missouri town.

He was finally allowed a "conjugal visit" as Colonel Jodzio termed it, two hours alone with Tammy in a tent. They cried, they kissed, and they held each other like all the husbands and wives did. When he tried to make love to her, she could not. Tammy Blevins had had enough (or perhaps too much) sex, and she was reluctant to be with her husband now.

"I am unclean," she said.

"You've been taken?" he asked.

She nodded, and cried.

He kissed away her tears and said, "I know it was not of your own free will. You aren't to blame. I forgive you, because you've done nothing wrong."

"You don't hate me?" his wife said.

"NO!" Maurice Blevins couldn't believe she'd say much a thing.

"You don't find me filthy?" she asked.

"Of course not."

Still, she could not bring herself to be with her husband.

Maurice Blevins could not sleep that night, ranting and raving about the injustice done to his woman, and how he would "chop off the dick" of every man who had touched her. While he kept some of the men from getting a good night's rest, no one told him to shut up, and no one could fault his angry words of desired revenge. Every man here felt the same way, including Judas Payne.

Judas wondered how he would feel if Evangeline were on the other side of the mountain. The notion made his chest and gut hurt. He would be like Mr. Blevins.

The next day, in the mines, without warning or preamble, Maurice Blevins raised his shoved and charged at the Jodzioite guard, screaming, "THIS IS FOR YOU TAMMY!"

Of course, before he could hit the guard with the shovel, the guard shot him straight in the face, blowing most of that angry expression away into a mess of bone, blood, and brain.

Another guard came rushing in, hearing the gun fire. They both looked down at the corpse.

"I know his wife well," the guard who shot him said, "she's terribly in love with me, and is a *screamer.*"

"Oh *her,*" the other guard said, "and I thought she was in love with *me!*"

They laughed, slapping each other on the back.

"What he did," Robert Kevin Scroggins said, "he did for love, and there's nothing more noble than that."

14.

Doña Maldita made a festivity of the matter, and all the whores at this particular brothel in Dallas, Texas, seemed to be having fun. Evangeline Payne wasn't having fun. This was a scene from Hell, and she started to believe that she had, in fact, died and been sent to Hell.

Men of all ages from Dallas, Austin, and Fort Worth came, as well as men from Mexico, who had received word of Maldita's auction for the virginity of the finest white whore she had ever acquired. Many of these men were skeptical, until Evangeline was brought before them: in a see-through, flowing white silk dress. Every man gazed upon her in astonishment—and Evangeline simply wanted to disappear into nothingness.

Maldita began the bid at two hundred dollars. Two hundred dollars! Evangeline could not image such money, and why a man would pay such—

But they were all very rich.

And in the end, the price was six hundred and fifty, going to a ruddy-faced, three hundred pound gentleman from Fort Worth, who must have been fifty or sixty years old.

The other whores cheering, this man hoisted Evangeline onto his shoulders. She kicked and hit him.

"A feisty one!" the man laughed. "This will be fun."

15.

Just as quickly as they had been taken into slave labor, one day all the captives were liberated—and by one man.

This man rode in like a fallen angel from the dust clouds of a forgotten heaven. He rode a brown and white spotted horse, wore a brown leather overcoat and a wide-brimmed black preacher's hat. He had a pistol in each hand, and four more tucked away in his belts, and two rifles on each side of his saddle, all Remington make.

He stormed in when the work shifts were over. As the men

left the mines, he entered the camp, firing his pistols. He was an excellent shot, never missing, killing the Jodzioites one by one with bullets straight in the middle of the eyes, or directly in their chests.

The Jodzioites from the other side rushed over to help in the battle, only to meet death.

All the men, tired from the day's work, watched in confusion.

The women ran over, worried about their husbands, hearing the sounds of battle.

Then it all stopped. There was a frightening silence. The man was still on his horse, unharmed, rifle now drawn, the fifteen Jodzioites dead.

"Be faithful until death," the man said in a loud, hollow voice, "and I will give you the crown of life." He paused. "Revelations, Chapter Two, Verse Ten."

"Malachi Brood." This came from Jodzio, who stood among his fallen men. He was unarmed, except for his saber.

The horseman smiled. "Charles K. Jodzio." He raised his rifle to the air. "Those who hate me without a cause are more than the hairs of my head; they are mighty who would destroy me, being my enemies wrongfully; though I have stolen nothing, I still must restore it. Psalms 69, Verse 4."

"The sun shall be turned into darkness, and the moon into blood," Jodzio said.

"Acts Two-Twenty," the man on the horse said, nodding.

"You have killed my men, Brood."

"They were good men, but not good enough."

"Why are you here?"

"I was hired," the man said. "Why else would I be here?"

"Who hired you to kill my men?" Jodzio said. "And are you going to kill me?"

"I was hired to kill no one, my old friend. I was hired to find a girl. The daughter of a wealthy Missouri businessman. It is my understanding she is here. It is my job to take her back to her father. I would not be able to do so if any of your men were alive."

"And me?"

"You may go if you wish. I'm here for the girl."

"I cannot allow this," Jodzio said.

"Then you shall die," the horseman said.

"It would be easy for you to kill me," the Colonel said. "You have that Remington, all I have is my sword. Could you, without your guns, fight me like a man?"

The horseman put his rifle away, and jumped off his horse. He placed his pistols on the ground.

"I would rather be a doorkeeper in the house of my God than dwell in the tents of wickedness. Psalms 84, Verse 10. I offer you this, Colonel: I shall fight you with my bare hands, and you can have your rapier. The odds are in your favor."

Jodzio didn't waste a moment. He cried out and charged at the man, but the man easily parried any attempts of being stabbed or sliced by Jodzio's blade. Every man and woman in the camp watched with enthralled attention. Quietly, and quickly unnoticed, the Negro and Chinese foremen left the scene, and fled the area, knowing their time here was through, and dangerous to stay.

Jodzio was sweating, breathing hard, exhausted with each lunge at the man in the coat and hat; the man was just to quick for him. Jodzio was exhausted after fifteen minutes.

"Give up, Charles," the man said, "while you still have your life."

"You have been a thorn in my side before," Jodzio said, "and now you have destroyed my operation and my plans! I will kill you—yes, this is what I shall do. *Let me kill you.*"

"When it is my time to die, God will call for me. Today is not that day, old friend."

"Lunatic! You're not even a real preacher!"

Jodzio went after him again, but this time the man grabbed Jodzio's wrist, pulled it up, along with the sword, and drove the end of the sword into Jodzio's stomach.

The man took the sword away.

Jodzio fell to his knees, his belly ripped open and bleeding.

The women became like a pack of furious, starving animals. In union, they howled and attacked Jodzio with their fists and feet, and then with rocks. What was left of the Colonel was a bloody pulp.

The men simply watched, many horrified by what their wives had become. But they watched in relish.

When the women were done, and stepped back in shame, their hands and faces covered in Jodzio's blood, the man spoke:

"My name is Father Malachi Brood. I am a man who is hired for certain difficult tasks. Who here is Tamara Blevins?"

A girl stepped forward, confused, and said, "I am Tammy Blevins, Mister."

"I have been sent by your father, a one Mr. Bernard Blevins." The girl wept. *"Father...."*

"When he heard that you didn't reach Santa Fe, nor any of the others in your group, he feared the worse. He thought it was Indians. I was referred to him. I said if you were alive, I would find you. It has taken me almost a month. But I have found you. And now I will take you back to your father, if you wish."

"If only you had been here a week sooner," she said, crying for her husband.

"The way of the wicked is like darkness," Father Malachi Brood said, looking away. "But the path of the just is like the shining sun. Proverbs...Four...18 and 19."

16.

It took a while for everyone in the camp to realize they were now free. They wanted to thank Brood, they wanted to shake and kiss his hand, give over the keys to their hearts and souls. This was not Brood's concern. He took one of the Jodzioites' horses, placed Tammy Blevins and her scant belongings on this horse, mounted his own steed, and rode off east, back to Missouri.

Now that they were all free, these people didn't know what

to do. Some wanted to continue to Santa Fe, others wanted to return home.

Judas Payne had no idea what he would do. He had no home to go back to, and he had no path to follow. He simply watched Malachi Brood ride off, wishing he was just like the man.

If I ever become anything, Judas thought, *I will be like him.*

No one in the camp realized, either, that with all the silver that had been collected, they were rich.

Robert Kevin Scroggins had not seen his wife in six weeks. He went to hug her. She did not return his hug. He felt it when his body was close to hers—she had changed since their last encounter.

Her stomach was slightly protruding. Not much, but it was noticeable.

"What happened?" he asked.

"I'm with child," she said, plainly.

"I..."

"One day I had no idea, then the next day...this," she said.

"I," Scroggins said again.

"Yes, it is his," Mary Jo said, looking at the meat that was once Colonel Charles K. Jodzio. "He was so proud of himself, the bastard. He wanted a son, of course, like any wretched man."

Robert was shaking; he said, *"You told me you had not been defiled!"*

"I hadn't, not by his men. Only by him." She sounded so cold, so matter-of-fact.

"How could you let him?!?" Robert cried.

Others hushed, drawn to the scene. The women looked down in shame. None of them were pregnant, but they could have been.

"Did I have a choice?" Mary Jo said. "He would have killed you."

He slapped her.

The women all gasped.

Mary Jo did not cry. Cheek red with the imprint of his hand, she glared at her husband.

"I did it for you," she said.

"Whore," he said. "You are no wife of mine. You are as good as dead." He turned, and walked away.

Judas said, "Robert, no—"

Robert Kevin Scroggins waved Judas away, and went into the tent where they had all been sleeping these past months.

Mary Jo Scroggins walked to the body of one of the Jodzioites and picked a pistol up. Before anyone could stop her, she placed the gun between her breasts and put a bullet into her broken heart.

CHAPTER FOUR

1.

Sheriff Paul Lish would wonder what his life would've been like had Evangeline Payne not suddenly, mysteriously, disappeared. The possibilities of different lives, different worlds, would haunt him at night and cause him to get little sleep. He would think about this during the day, too—he would tell himself: "It simply ain't fair." What could he do? He couldn't go up against Tyburn's preacher, the good citizens would turn against him and come election time, he wouldn't have a job. And that just would not do. Paul Lish was a man of the law, and without the law he'd have no life, he might as well just put a bullet into his brain.

2.

Evangeline would sometimes think about the Sheriff and the probability of being his wife. In the beginning, when strange men would do to do her what they paid for, she would close her eyes and pretend she was with Paul Lish. After a while she couldn't maintain this fantasy; the men she fucked were large and hairy and stank and didn't treat her nicely, not the way she knew Paul Lish would've been kind to her. What happened in the bedroom with the whorehouse "clients" was not love-making, this much she was certain. Each day, she grew to hate men and their horrid desires. Six days a week, she went to bed with anywhere from five to twenty-five men *a day*. Maldita's clients really liked her, too—she was new, she was young, she was fresh, and she was pretty. That's what she heard an awful lot: "I cain't believe how prettah you is, missy." These men may have been mesmerized by whatever beauty she possessed, but they didn't treat her like a delicate flower once in the bed. Evangeline seemed to attract the attention of those fellows with odd peccadilloes—they liked to slap her across the face or on her rear end while having sex; they liked to pull her hair or bite her on the neck; they liked to put their members or bottles of whiskey inside the place where she defalcated, and that always hurt or made her bleed. "You must *learn* to like it," Maldita always told her, "or do a damn good job pretending," but Evangeline Payne vowed to never enjoy anything that happened in the whorehouse, even if it was "normal making love" and the men would whisper, "I love you, girl" into her ear while they did to her what they paid money for.

Twice, Evangeline knew she was with child and, of course, she had no idea who the father was. She was both disgusted and delighted by the notion of giving birth. Doña Maldita knew a "doctor"—an old man who was once a Confederate medical officer—who would take care of the whores if they became pregnant.

Evangeline was given laudanum and the baby bloodily removed. These situations always angered Maldita, because her whores would be out of commission for several days to a week after.

"Make sure they do not shoot their seed inside of you," Maldita told Evangeline.

"I tell them not to, but sometimes they just do it. They say they forget."

"Then when you know they are about to shoot, push yourself away from them. Every day you can't work is a day I lose money. Do you understand the implications of that, young woman?"

Evangeline nodded and said, "Yes, ma'am, I do."

3.

As for Judas Payne, the young man wandered about the western part of the nation as men did in those days, living, as they say, "hand-to-mouth" and moving about like a wraith; after a year, he eventually found himself in the small town of Bell, Arizona, working his daylight hours as a copper miner. His skills as a slave laborer for Jodzio and his men earned him a quick position, but any man, he knew, could break his back digging into the earth.

He had no idea how he got there, but there he was, and this was his life, if one could call it a life.

He was making money, but he wasn't very good at keeping it, and that didn't seem to matter. Many best plans would go to hell with drink and women; money was lost at the card tables; men who put their earnings in the bank were never sure how safe it would be, as the bank was robbed at least once a month and no one ever seemed to be caught or the money retrieved (there was rumor that the robbers were working with the government and the heisted dollars going back to Washington).

Weekends were the busiest, and the most rowdy and dangerous, during the weekends in the bustling town of Jerome, Arizona. The saloons and whorehouses didn't close; men could be found passed out, near dead from too much whiskey and near broke from an overindulgence in sex and gambling. On Sundays, few went to church to seek forgiveness; there was a small, make-shift tabernacle, yes, and a preacher, but few men around cared about the judgments of God.

Monday morning, the men were back in the mines in pursuit of wages and riches.

Judas was among them, and this is where he befriended an odd sort of man, a fellow named Arthur Brooke. Right off, Judas knew that Brooke didn't belong here—not just in this mine but this world, it seemed. He'd also seen Brooke praying in the tent with the preacher and felt sorry for the man, that he'd turn to such a thing.

Trust no preacher, he wanted to tell people, *my father was one, and I can tell you some horrible tales...*

Judas knew that if he ever said such a thing, there would be men who would want to hurt, or even kill, him.

It was a dumb man, he thought, who mocked the rigorous religious beliefs of other men.

When asked, "Do you believe in God, sir?" Judas Payne always lied: "But of course."

"Do you believe in Jesus, mister?"

The answer: "In the very baby Jesus, my brother."

"Praise be! This one-eyed man is saved!"

It made life easier to lie.

So, one drunken night, when Arthur Brooke asked, "Do you believe in God?" Judas smirked, and then he laughed, because it was the last thing he thought Brooke would inquire.

Brooke smiled and drank from his bottle of whiskey. "That's how I feel," he said, "because I don't believe there's no fucking God and I should know better."

"Why should you know better?"

"Because I have seen many wonders, my friend, there are things *I know* that you would never believe."

"You talk strange at times," Judas said.

"This I know," Brooke said.

So the two drank and in the morning they worked in the mines. This was their life in Bell, Arizona, and while it wasn't the best life a man could have, it was preferable to Judas' days gone by.

4.

When Evangeline had sex with Maldita's customers, she would keep her eyes shut and (like Sheriff Lish) think about all the possible lives she could have had. She would leave her body, would not feel what was being done to it, travel to other cities, states, countries and worlds. Sometimes, her dear brother was there with her, but most of the time he was as lost as she.

One night, she had a certain special visitor. She didn't know how certain or special this fellow was, because he was THE DEVIL himself—and she didn't know he was THE DEVIL because he appeared like a man. Not like most men—all those ruffians and grimy cowboys who never knew how to handle a woman, whore or not—because he wore a suit and a stove-top hat, walked with a cane; he was handsome and his eyes seemed to glow. "I paid the Madame of the house all night for you," he said as he walked into her room.

"Why me?" she asked timidly. "I don't believe we have met."

"We have not," said the man. "But I know you're the prettiest girl in the entire house. That's the word on the street."

She said, "What is your name, mister? If I may ask."

"What's in a name? Names do not matter. Why don't you get naked?"

She did this.

"Nice," said THE DEVIL, touching her pale flesh. He caressed her and kissed her. Evangeline liked this, because it was so different—this man didn't demand she take his penis in her mouth right away like most of them did. He didn't want immediate sex. He touched her all over her body and this sent tingles up and down her spine. He smelled her hair. "You smell like your mother," said THE DEVIL.

She didn't know what he meant. Before she could say anything, his gentility stopped and he began to slap her across the face.

"Take that, whore!"

He hit her over and over.

She tasted a lot of blood, she knew her jaw was broken. she had lost some teeth. One of her eyes was swollen shut. The man flipped her over on her belly, twisted her arm back and broke it. The snap of her bones echoed in the room. Her face was shoved into the pillow so her screams were muffled. She felt the man enter her rear end. Her world was pain. The man leaned down and whispered into her ear: "I raped your mother too but you're so much better, you're so much dirty, you ain't nothin' but a worthless piece of cow dung, you filthy whore."

Then he was gone.

She was left there, in her own blood and feces.

It took a while to get up. She didn't know what part of her body was in more pain—probably her broken arm. Her face was mostly numb.

She looked in the mirror with the one good eye and tried to scream. She could not scream because of her broken jaw—

5.

—she did scream, a yelp really, and she sat up in bed. There was no pain. Her arm was all right. She touched her face—her face was fine. She went to the mirror. She was not injured. What a strange dream, she thought.

In the mirror, she saw him standing behind her.

The well-dressed, handsome man.

She turned around.

"You," she said.

"Don't be frightened," he said.

Evangeline shook her head.

"I paid good money for you," the man said, his eyes looking red, "so get undressed and let's make love...again."

6.

Evangeline woke up in the morning and she was fine, all that violence had been in her imagination. The man who'd hurt her all night and told her how he was once her mother's lover did not exist. She knew she must've been going mad....

And THE DEVIL, he laughed deep inside her heart, a place he could now call home.

7.

Often, Judas Payne thought about the mysterious gunslinger that had saved him from Jodzio's enslavement. Where was the man, where did he come from? Judas would like to find him and learn from the man, perhaps do the same kind of work, rather than busting his back in a copper mine.

He also thought about his half-sister a lot. He knew she was in distress, for their hearts were connected. One night he had a disturbing dream that their father, the pious Reverend Payne, made his way into her bedroom and had carnal knowledge with her. He got on top of her and held her down and...raped her. Judas woke from this dream crying and sweating.

"Evangeline," he whispered....

8.

...and at the same time, Evangeline, in her room at the brothel, late at night, woke up sweating from a dream she had that Judas was in a jail cell and being tortured by demons with pitch forks.

"Judas," she whispered, "oh Judas, where are you? If I could only help you, and you could help me."

9.

She needed help more than ever before. The mysterious stranger who had beat her had left his mark on her, both on her body and in her soul. Word got around that she was the type of whore who liked to be man-handled and enjoyed the rough, so she started to get customers who would slap and punch her and when she cried, they'd say, "I was told you enjoy this sort of thing," and they'd add: "Because I sure do, and it's hard to find a whore who will take a beatin' and ask for more."

It was Maldita herself who had been spreading the word that the whore Evangeline could be bruised and sullied. Maldita decided this was the best way to make money from the girl who was now a deformity when it came to whores. Evangeline now walked with a pronounced limp; and her arm had not been set in a cast correctly (by a drunken doctor who happened to be at the brothel the night Evangeline was attacked), so the arm had an odd bent to it. Evangeline's nose had been broken in two places, plus her jaw, and she had several scars across her once-beautiful place. To make matters worse, the girl wasn't eating much properly, and she lost weight, so she was scrawny now, her rib cage sticking out, and her skin had lost its glow because she was drinking too much alcohol as well. The whiskey, rye and bourbon helped Evangeline go to sleep each night, or helped her endure a beating or sodomy; booze also helped her forgot many things that were painful to ponder on, as many who have turned to the drink come to find out. 100 proof was perfect for numbing memory and soul.

When Evangeline protested the type of men she was sent to bed with, to entertain their vile need to hurt a woman, Maldita simply told the girl: "I paid good money for you and no one will pay good money for a whore that looks like you no do, except for those gentlemen with specific needs and requests."

"They're all pigs!" said Evangeline.

Maldita laughed at that. "Chica, *all* men are swine, haven't you figured that out yet? Even your own father, a man of the cloth, is a rotten animal."

Not my brother, he's not a beast, she thought. Judas is an angel, and that's what he'll always be in my heart and mind...

10.

With his hard-earned money, Judas Payne purchased two pistols: a Remington for his right hand, and a Smith and Wesson for his left. He wasn't aware of it, but his father THE DEVIL was whispering in his ear about which choice to make. "Each gun fits a purpose for what hand you choose to use," muttered THE DEVIL.

For months he practiced shooting, alone in the desert, firing at bottles, cacti, and the occasional tree. With his one eye, he became a pretty good shot. It was only until he thought he was ready that Judas decided to go "home" to Kentucky.

Running and hiding was not the answer, not for him and not for any man. Like the gunslinger he had come to admire, a man confronted issues, sometimes with six-bullets leading the way.

He would go home and rescue his dear sister, and then he would deal with the good Reverend in whatever manner seemed appropriate at the time. Judas Payne knew that just about anything could happen....

11.

His first test, whether he could be a man with a gun in his life or not, came three days after setting out for Tyburn, Kentucky. Alone on a trail in New Mexico, near sunset, he was approached by three grubby-looking Comancheros who pointed rifles at him and told him he was being robbed.

"I don't have much to steal," Judas said.

"You have a fine horse and those two pistols on your belt," one of them said in strained English. "And I know you must have a few dollars tucked away. Your boots look new. I need some new boots myself, amigo."

"That would leave me nothing," Judas said, "barefoot out here under the hot sun."

Off to the side, THE DEVIL watched this.

"Take it easy, boy," said THE DEVIL, "take your time, take a deep breath, and then kill these fools!"

And that is what Judas Payne did.

Before the Comancheros could react or say another word, Judas quickly pulled his pistols out, one in each hand, and fired several times.

Two of the robbers got a bullet straight between the eyes, killing them instantly; the third got a bullet in the neck, opening up an artery, blood sprouting out in a fountain of red...a second bullet got him in the nose, and bore its way into the robber's gray matter.

Judas took one of the rifles. It might come in handy. He also took all their bullets, and the money they had on their body, which amounted to twenty-two dollars. That would come in handy too.

He had to qualms about stealing from the dead, because they would have done the same.

"Good, good," said THE DEVIL in the wind, "I am proud of you, boy!"

Nothing was going to stop Judas from what he had to, *needed* to do.

He rode on....

CHAPTER FIVE

1.

The Revered Jedediah Payne did not expect the creature that walked through his door. He was in the kitchen having breakfast and then it came in: that one-eyed hell-spawn.

"You," said the Reverend, "what are you doing here in *my* home?"

"I came for my sister," Judas said to the man he once called his father.

The Reverend laughed.

Judas pulled out one of his pistols.

"How dare you point a weapon at me!"

"Evangeline. Where is she?"

"She's none of your concern."

Judas fired. The bullet nicked the Reverend's left ear, taking a small piece of flesh with it, and lodged into the kitchen wall.

The Reverend placed a hand at his ear, feeling pain, feeling blood oozing down his neck.

"You missed."

"I'm a good shot," Judas said. "I won't miss the spot between your eyes next time, unless you tell me where my sister is."

Again, the Reverend laughed.

Judas aimed.

"I'll tell you," said the Reverend, and he did. He relished the look of horror expressed in the hell-spawn's one good eye. "She's where she belongs, where all whores belong..."

2.

It was a three day ride to the Texas town where the brothel was located. Judas didn't sleep much. He would not sleep until she was safe in his arms.

In the town, he wasted no time, heading straight for the brothel.

He walked in, ready.

A woman greeted him. She was half-clothed. When she asked what his pleasure was, Judas Payne said, "I know no pleasure. All I want is my sister."

"You're funny, mister," the woman said. She stopped giggling when Judas pulled out his two pistols.

3.

Doña Maldita was sitting in her room, reading the Bible, when she heard the sounds of gunshots in the parlor. She jumped up, put on a robe, and ran out. The whores throughout the brothel were screaming. She saw that both her bodyguards were dead and bleeding, lying on the floor, and a man with dark skin and one eye, holding two guns, stood above their bodies.

"You, lady," the man said to her, "are you the madam of this... establishment?"

"Who are you?" she cried. "What have you done?!"

He pointed a pistol at her. "I won't ask again. Are you the madam?"

"Sí," Maldita said, shaking, "yes."

"Evangeline Payne," he said coldly, "where is she?"

4.

Evangeline Payne was asleep when she heard the gunshots downstairs. She had been sleeping hard, exhausted from having serviced nearly fifteen men the night before. She heard the screams, the sounds of bullets, and then silence.

She knew something bad and evil had arrived at the brothel. She always knew a day like this would come. She would ready for anything; she was prepared to die.

She heard loud footsteps coming up the stairs...the jangling of spurs...the sound of a pistol cocked...

The Devil is coming for me, she thought.

She did not know THE DEVIL himself was already in her room, waiting in the shadows, watching to see what would transpire.

THE DEVIL grinned and said, "Come to her, my bastard son."

The bedroom door opened...

There stood a dark figure.

"Evangeline," a man's voice said.

She knew that voice! A voice from her dreams, a voice from her past, another life...

"Evangeline," the figure said again, and stepped forward.

"Judas?" she said. "Is that you?"

"Yes, yes," he said, and it was him. He rushed to her and held her in his arms. "I've found you."

"Am I dreaming?" she asked.

"No."

"How can this be?"

"I looked everywhere for you," he told her, "I thought of this day every day in my head..."

"Judas!" she cried, and held him tight.

"We must go now."

She realized he was looking at her, and she was horrified by what she knew he saw: a damaged whore, used and tortured by men of all ages, all persuasions...

"Don't look at me," she said.

"It doesn't matter, Evangeline."

"What you must think of me," she said.

"It doesn't matter...quickly, we have to leave...."

5.

She held onto his arm as they walked down the stairs, since she could not walk properly after the healing of her many injuries.

At the bottom of the stairs, Maldita was loading a shotgun, intent on killing them both.

Judas killed her first.

A bullet between the eyes.

Evangeline smiled...she had fantasized of Maldita's death, in many horrible ways, and it seemed fitting that she meet her doom at the hands of her angel, her brother.

6.

THE DEVIL followed them.

He followed them out of the brothel. He followed them as they ride out of town on a horse.

He followed them out into the desert of the West...

...all the while whispering terrible things into Evangeline's ear:

"You are a worthless filthy whore and he knows it."

"You are disgusting and have no reason to live."

"He will leave you because you are dirty."

7.

They set up camp under the stars. Judas started a fire. They held each other and kissed each other and no matter what Judas said, what promises of love he told her, Evangeline was ashamed for all she had done, for the way she looked and smelled, all those men...hundreds of men over the years...men who broke her body, men who stole her soul....

8.

Judas slept but she could not. The Devil was at her side, telling her to do it, do it, it was for the best, just do it....

So she did it.

She got up and went to her brother.

She took one of his guns....

9.

Judas woke up but he was too late to stop her.

Evangeline had his Remington pistol pointed to her head.

"What are you doing?"

"I'm sorry, my darling," Evangeline Payne said, pulling the trigger and doing what Mary Jo Scroggins had done, to erase the shame and end the torment.

THE DEVIL laughed.

10.

THE DEVIL laughed as he sat in the church pews and listened to the lies Reverend Payne pontificated to the twenty men and women who sat and listened.

The Reverend stopped speaking.

The doors to the church opened, and in walked that heathen creature.

"For you see now," cried the Reverend, "Satan has sent one of his vile hell spawn to quiet the words of the Lord!"

"THE DEVIL sent me all right," said the man who walked in the church, the man known as Judas Payne, the man who, before twenty witnessed, shot and killed the Reverend, "in cold blood and one eye," as the story would go, the beginning of a myth...

Judas looked over at THE DEVIL when the deed was done.

"Good, good, very good," said THE DEVIL with a laugh.

11.

Sheriff Paul Lish was in the church and was just as shocked as anyone to see this stranger saunter into a House of God and murder a man of the cloth.

Lish ran after the one-eyed killer, reaching for his holstered gun, to shoot or arrest the culprit.

Lish didn't have a chance.

Lish was shot dead on the steps leading into the church.

THE DEVIL stepped over his dead body.

12.

Cold, without emotion and a frozen soul, Judas Payne rode his horse out of Tyburn, Kansas, hell close behind him.

And a weird western legend began....

ABOUT THE AUTHOR

Michael Hemmingson writes books in every possible genre he can: literary, western, SF, horror, noir, autobiography, erotica, narrative journalism, gonzo journalism, cultural anthropology, critical theory, critifiction, ethnography, and poetry. And private eye yarns. And film and TV studies. He also writes plays and screenplays. He wrote the independent feature film, *The Watermelon*, which you can get on Netflix or Amazon.

www.ingramcontent.com/pod-product-compliance
Lightning Source LLC
Chambersburg PA
CBHW021239260626
47155CB00004BA/1215

WEBB'S WEIRD WILD WEST

In Don *Webb's Weird Wild West*, Henry James avenges his brother Jesse, Robert E. Howard's serpent people are a modern gang, Satan flies a Zeppelin, and hobos liberate a zebra from a stolen train.

"Don Webb can write straight tales or he can go out to the fringe, where the cutting edge hasn't even cut yet, [where he] plays head-churning games and word games: [he's] a full spectrum writer."

—Roger Zelazny

Borgo Press Books by DON WEBB

Do the Weird Crime, Serve the Weird Time
The War with the Belatrin
Webb's Weird Wild West: Western Tales of Horror

WEBB'S WEIRD WILD WEST

WESTERN TALES OF HORROR

DON WEBB

THE BORGO PRESS

MMXI

WEBB'S WEIRD WILD WEST

FIRST EDITION

Published by Wildside Press LLC

www.wildsidebooks.com

DEDICATION

For Gardner Dozois,

Who Gave Me Tons of Confidence

CONTENTS

ACKNOWLEDGMENTS

These stories were previously published as follows, and are reprinted (with some editing, updating, and textual modifications) with the permission of the author:

"Jesse Revenged" in *Isaac Asimov's Science Fiction Magazine*, Vol. 10, No. 12 (Dec 1986); reprinted in *Isaac Asimov's SF-Lite* Bantam-Doubleday-Dell (1993). Copyright © 1986, 1993, 2011 by Don Webb.

"A Note to His Publisher" in the hardback anthology, *Copper Star*, distributed as part of the 1991 World Fantasy Convention. Copyright © 1991, 2011 by Don Webb.

"Seven Four Planting" in a limited edition surplus book with *The Bestseller and Other Stories*, Chris Drumm Books (1993). Copyright © 1993, 2011 by Don Webb.

"Innocents Abroad" in *Blood from Stones* (Fall 1999). Copyright © 1999, 2011 by Don Webb.

"A Half-Dime Adventure" in *Isaac Asimov's Science Fiction Magazine*, Vol. 14, No 10 (Oct. 1990). Copyright © 1990, 2011 by Don Webb.

"Billy Hauser" in *Isaac Asimov's Science Fiction Magazine*, Vol. 15, No. 14 (December 1991). Copyright © 1991, 2011 by Don Webb.

"Common Superstitions" in *Isaac Asimov's Science Fiction Magazine*, Vol. 12, No. 10 (Oct. 1988). Copyright © 1988, 2011 by Don Webb.

"Sabbath of the Zeppelins" in *Asimov's Science Fiction*

JESSE REVENGED

The community of Oneida had become Amarillo, Tascosa was beginning to fade into the dust, and a few weeks ago Admiral Sampson blockaded the navy of Admiral Cervera in Santiago Bay. It was the summer of 1898. Robert Ford, the man who shot Jesse James in the back, had left the Ozarks and moved to Amarillo. He lived in the third floor of the yellow-painted wooden Amarillo Hotel. He'd changed his name to Aubrey Sorrentino and affected an Italian accent.

He sits on the wide porch of the Amarillo and slowly fans himself. Lesser men would've been blinded by the gleam from his refulgent ebon leather boots. But Aubrey sits with his boots up, face lit by the black light, and sips very slowly a Texas Tumbleweed.

Aubrey doesn't know that his doom is already coming by train from California.

He's plotting how to extend his hotel bill. Maybe he'll borrow money from a wealthy rancher using his phony Count title and his phony Old World charm. The reward money from shooting Jesse seventeen years ago has long since been converted to wine, women, and song. He'll have another cigar by and by.

Heavy rain last night and the ridiculous wooden cobbles the city bought in the spring have begun to swell. Every now and then one pops out of the grid shooting eight or ten feet into the air. The horses hitched in front of the hotel are getting a mite skittish. Aubrey wishes it were cooler.

In California having completed his lecture on philosophical conceptions and practical results William James boarded an eastbound train. His brother Henry had arrived a week before ostensibly to autograph copies of just-released In the Cage at a Navajo bookstore in nearby Arizona. They had a private car.

William didn't speak to Henry until they passed through Tombstone. He'd just corrected proofs of *Human Immortality*. He was still peeved at Henry for siding with Frank and against him on the ideas of the specious present. In Tombstone he recited the James brothers creed to break the silence, "Never rob from a friend, a Southerner, a preacher, or a widow. Amen."

"Amen," said Henry.

Henry opened up a small hand-tooled leather valise. Inside were two pairs of pearl-handled revolvers. One pair had been Jesse's, the other was Frank's who was too old for this. Henry handed Jesse's guns to William.

William said, "I see you're already interested in the dense symbolism and complicated characterization that will come to dominate your later work."

Henry nodded grimly.

As the warm stars of the Panhandle night begin to shine through the lavender and orange Texas sunset, Aubrey makes his way to his room. He opens his last bottle of Kentucky bourbon and dips his pen in the inkwell the Chinese boy had brought. The two civilizing claims that the six-year-old city of Amarillo has are a five-story hotel and two Chinese gofers, Joe Fong Yang and Joe Fong Yin. Aubrey begins the 37th chapter of his autobiography, Robert Ford My Story. Aubrey writes, "To Carthage I come, where a cauldron of unholy loves sang about my ears. Since I had developed elephantiasis in my testicles six months ago in New Orleans I was tone-deaf. So I went to Amarillo." He is referring to Carthage, Texas but the words—at least the first string of them—are St. Augustine's. The man who shot Jesse James in the back is not above plagiarism. Aubrey takes a long swig of bourbon and decides to stretch his legs. He locks his bio carefully away in a Confederate Army strongbox.

When Aubrey reaches the door of the Amarillo no more sunset remains. He walks toward the depot, a thousand schemes hatching in his brain. A swarthy man lights a kerosene lamp in front of a buffalo hide tent.

MADAME ROSA
Reader and Adviser
Palm—Head—Cards Read

The tent's new. The hides smell and look a little stiff. Aubrey walks up to the swarthy man. "How much?"

"Palm read ten cents. Head read ten cents. Cards read fifteen cents. Triple reading thirty cents."

Aubrey hands the man a quarter and a nickel. The man sticks his head through the folds and says, "Triple reading." Aubrey enters. The man walks up the street toward the saloon.

Rosa an ancient and enigmatic gypsy quietly and efficiently does the three readings. Across the candles she stares sad and sullen at the elderly stranger. Finally she says, "You've got troubles."

"Like what?"

"Like death. I can see in your palm that someone's coming to kill you. Someone influenced by the novels of Ivan Turgenev. Someone who's an excellent marksman and a damn fine writer."

Aubrey feels his bowels turn into cold aspic. He's naked without a gun belt. But he still appreciates the value of money, he'll get his thirty cents worth. He asks Rosa, "This someone, does he come alone?"

"No. I feel he's traveling with an older bearded man. An older

man who distrusts all monistic absolutisms."

"Anyone else?"

"No. Just the two. Coming from the direction of the setting sun."

Aubrey knew the first man was Henry, the writer. The second could be either Frank or William. Both were good shots— maybe as good as Jesse. He couldn't remember if the subject of monistic absolutisms came up when they were planning bank jobs.

"Are they going to kill me?"

"They'll try. I think the younger one will succeed."

"But it's not certain?"

"Mister, if I thought the future was fixed, would I charge thirty cents trying to help people avoid it?"

Aubrey is relieved.

Outside the tent another wooden cobble rockets into the air.

The train stops around midnight to take on water and coal near the eastern Arizona border. Henry awakens. He's forgotten the photographer. Dammit. He'd promised John Singer Sargent pictures of the shootout. Henry wonders if they should call the whole thing off. They've done that too often waiting to the end of this novel or that book. Maybe they can hire a photographer in Amarillo. The train begins rolling.

Aubrey Sorrentino buys the swarthy man another watered whiskey. Four drunk cowpokes simulate a poker game near the saloon door. Aubrey shows the Romani a wad of bills. The outer bills are U.S. currency, the inner and more numerous are Confederate boodle. The Romani chai smiles and pulls a knife from his belt. He plunges the knife into a photo of Henry James laying on their wobbly table. The chai has bad teeth. Aubrey buys the man a bottle and then heads back to his hotel.

Aubrey's sleep is fitful but no more fitful than any night since he shot Jesse. Phantoms of the remaining James brothers appear every night. Sometimes singly. Sometimes the whole gang: Frank James, William James, Henry James, Josiah Royce, Herman von Helmholtz, Ford Maddox Ford, and Doc Holiday.

They'd had their petty revenges over the years, but now they were going for hot lead. Aubrey's cheeks still burned at the thought of Henry's devastating review of Aubrey's first novel Missouri Christmas in the North American Review. That review had closed publishers' doors on two continents. He'd show them. He'd kept in shape and could outshoot all of them except maybe Frank or Henry.

The train pulls into Amarillo about an hour after dawn. The gypsy waits in the shadow of the depot. The James brothers step down. They travel light, only a bag apiece. Their eyes are as cold as an Amarillo winter. The gypsy draws his bowie knife, presses himself flat against the wooden frame of the station. The James brothers talk. William's going to rent a room. Henry's going to try getting a photographer. William walks southward and Henry walks northward, gypsy-ward.

The gypsy shifts slightly preparing to spring. Henry's predator hearing informs him. Henry drops the suitcase and jumps around the depot's corner facing the gypsy. The gypsy lunges but Henry's gun is quicker. A bright red rose blooms in the gypsy's chest. Henry asks the falling man if he knows of any photographers working in the Amarillo area, but it is too late. Henry pauses to cut another notch in his pistol grip.

The dining room of the Amarillo Hotel opens onto the main lobby. Aubrey sits, back against the wall, watching the lobby and shoveling down biscuits and gravy. Aubrey chokes as William walks in. William turns without breaking his stride and flashes Aubrey a huge smile. Aubrey knows how George Armstrong Custer, old Yellow Hair himself, felt when he looked up the canyon walls at Little Bighorn.

William signs in. The manager says, "Gee, Mr. James, it's an honor to have you and your brother here. I surely enjoyed *The Will to Believe and Other Essays in Popular Philosophy*."

"Thanks," says William.

William pages back through the hotel's register until he finds Aubrey Sorrentino. He draws a line through the name and writes in Robert Ford. He pushes the register back to the manager.

The manager's eyes widen but he says nothing only (and almost imperceptibly) nods.

Robert Ford runs up to his room for the security of his guns. Later on he will almost shoot a chambermaid.

William makes himself comfortable in his fourth floor room. He sips on the glass of buttermilk he'd got in the dining room. About eleven Henry comes in. From Henry's haggard hangdog look, William knows there's not a photographer to be had.

When noon comes the James brothers go to the wide porch of the hotel. William pulls a revolver and motions everybody off the street. It's quiet and hot. William steps into the street and shouts, "Robert Ford, I am calling you out."

The waiting is intolerable.

Then Ford appears in an all-black outfit. His black Stetson is edged with Mexican silver. He walks calmly out of the hotel, nodding amicably to Henry who sets on a bench. He steps off the porch. His eyes lock on William with rattlesnake intensity.

He goes for his gun.

As William goes for his gun, one of the rain-soaked wooden cobbles shoots into the air between him and Ford. William shoots the cobble. He has a flash of *satori* concerning human cognitive processes.

Robert isn't distracted. His bullet tears into William just below the rib cage.

Robert wheels and fires at Henry. Henry's on his feet shooting. Robert misses. Henry doesn't.

Henry runs to his dying brother.

Henry says, "William, you've got to make it."

"I'm a goner. But we got him. We got Ford."

"I don't want to lose two brothers to Ford."

"Get Frank out of retirement. Get him to take up my career so I can be remembered. In my bag I've got some notes on the variety of religious experience he should find invaluable." William's breathing stops.

Henry stands. The silence is deafening.

A NOTE TO HIS PUBLISHER

George Catlin
St. Louis
American Territory

W. O. Thule
Egyptian House
Piccadilly, London

Dear W. O.,

I am further along in writing my book than I had imagined I would be by now. So you'll be glad to know that a copperplate of the MSS. will be coming your way in a few months. I have only one sticking point.

Something happened in the Yellowstone.

No other white man saw this. I have fought with myself for months between vowing to tell it or to keep it to myself forever. I will tell it to you because you are far away in London, and that smoky city doesn't seem real to me as I pen these lines. Some parts of this tale will appear in my book, but those parts at the end of my tale—those things which run contrary to the "laws" of Nature—- I will tell to you alone. It begins with Wi-jun-jon.

Wi-jun-jon of the Assinneboin arrived in St. Louis from the Yellowstone, a journey of some two thousand miles by Mackinaw boat, and I was on the docks to receive him. His wild

beauty I attempted to capture in paint. He was a striking figure: his leggings and shirt were of the mountain-goat skin, richly garnished with quills of porcupine, and fringed with locks of scalps, taken from enemies' heads. Over these floated his long hair in plaits, that fell nearly to the ground; his head was decked with the war eagle's plumes and his robe was young buffalo bull. His quiver and bow were slung and he bore war club and a *par flèche* shield, made of bull's neck skin. His bearing was proud, but in the depths of his eyes were fear for what lay ahead; although I credit myself as the only white man who could read those eyes. Mr. Chouteau of the American Fur Company was on hand, and he asked me the meaning of Wi-jun-jon and I translated from the Sioux tongue, "Pigeon's egg head" and this was the cause of much laughter.

Wi-jun-jon had a companion whose name I did not learn. But this companion sought me out in the night—I being one of the three persons out of the 15,000 St. Louisians, who could speak Sioux. Although his dialect differed greatly from the Lakota Sioux—mainly in its inclusion of Cree—it provided me with useful practice. He told me that Wi-jun-jon and himself had set out to make a census of white men. They had already met French fur traders and the German-speaking founder of the American Fur Company, Prince Maximilian of Wied-Neuwied, but they wondered at the number of the English-speaking tribe. So they began cutting notches in a pipe. There were few cabins in the first hundred miles, but as river met river they filled the pipe and began to notch his war club. Soon that too was full and they were beginning to worry at the number of notches. One night when the fur traders had tied up the boat, they went ashore and cut a long birch stick. This they filled more and more until they neared St. Louis. When they saw the great camp they threw the stick in the Missouri. This companion asked if I thought there were many more of the English-speaking tribe, and I gravely replied many, many more. Whereupon he said that he would return home, because his mind would be too full of white men.

Wi-jun-jon did not take his companion's counsel. He would

bravely see what was about to engulf his people. So he journeyed to see cities and guns and balloons and other wonders. I would see him again in the spring.

It was a cold and hard winter—many in the city took influenza. I was feverish, but only in my desire to paint. Mr. Chouteau purchased a steamboat for the American Fur Company, and I spent many evenings there planning for our expedition in the spring. I heard rumors of Wi-jun-jon. He had made his speech to the President. He had visited the theatre, he had ridden a balloon in Philadelphia.

He returned on the first of April taking up residence in the ship's hull—overseeing the trade goods, which were destined for his people. I was greatly curious to see him, but he did not put on deck until we had cast away.

He was indeed a sorry spectacle. Puss in boots.

The President had presented him with a military costume—broadcloth of the finest blue trimmed with lace of gold; on his shoulders were mounted immense epaulettes; his neck was strangled with a shining black stock; and his feet were pinioned in a pair of waterproof boots, with high heels. He walked uneasily—"stepping like a yoked hog."

Washington had crowned him with an immense beaver hat, which flashed a broad silver lace band, and was surmounted by a huge red feather, some two feet high. His coat collar, stiff with lace, came higher up than his ears, and over it flowed, down towards his haunches, his long Indian locks stuck up in rolls and plaits with red paint. He wore a large silver medal on a blue ribbon about his neck, and across his right shoulder a wide belt to support a broad sword. He wore white kid gloves to carry his two prize possessions—in his right hand a blue umbrella and in his left a large ladies' fan.

He saw me and smiled, mistaking my laughter for good cheer. He strutted up to me stiff as a cob on a spindle. He demonstrated the final mark of his metamorphosis. He had been taught to whistle, "Yankee Doodle." I knew I would have to paint him. I had made a sketch in the fall, but there would have to be two

facing plates in my book. I completed both paintings during the two thousand mile trip to the Yellowstone.

He disembarked among his people and began to tell them of the wonders he had seen, while I began taking in wonders of the grizzly bear and the geyser. I will have to rely on my Assiniboine informants for the first part of my tale; although I was there at the end.

The Assiniboine listened with great interest until the tally stick was thrown in the Missouri. The rest was clearly fiction. The whites are great liars, he had caught their sickness. Despite growing disbelief, Wi-jun-jon continued his tale—flying like a bird over Philadelphia. The chiefs after three nights began to shun him. He lost his political eminence, but the gossiping members of the tribe were open to him. Each night the campfire circle and wigwam fireside audience grew.

He divided his bounty among his relatives. His laced frock was converted into a much-admired pair of leggings for his wife (which were topped by silver lace garters courtesy of the beaver hat!). His white linen shirt somehow found its way to a young woman, who had listened to his stories with an extreme wide-eyed interest. His pantaloons, blue and white with gold lace trim, were the next to go—razored into leggings for another "catch crumb." The umbrella alone remained after this disassemblage (the fan having been spirited away by a jealous wind).

Despite his grave demonstrations with the umbrella his stories continued to be disbelieved. He seemed however content to lecture and had an inexhaustible source. He had visited seventy-four gun ships, seen the great council house of the white men (Congress), he had seen the patent office with its wondrous and curious machines and this he averred to be the greatest medicine place on earth.

However his audience grew and not only Assiniboine. Nearby Mandans and Cree came. Translators whispered in the echoes of his whispers. Sometimes gifts were left.

In some his tales induced an excitement. Their lives had lost some of their sheen. Particularly the young boys about to

become braves and the middle-aged men and women, who were finding themselves "in the midst of the forest dark" as Dante says. Many enjoyed working to the accompaniment—braves would dehair buffalo for their *par flèche* shields, oil their rifles, fletch their arrows.

As the crowds grew so did talk among the chiefs. The only similar phenomena was the Bull Dance of the Mandans. And after the dance did not the elusive herds come near the Mandan villages? Perhaps Wi-jun-jon's tale would draw these wonders. They had never seen a steam boat until Wi-jun-jon brought one. Perhaps his lies were creating these things. After much consultation the chiefs decided to honor him as a medicine man.

The chiefs so hailed him. Now his tales were no longer mere amusements, but medicine. Some openly hailed him as the greatest of medicine for the wonderful alacrity with which he created his lies. That he should be the greatest of medicine, and that for lying, merely, rendered him a prodigy in mysteries that commanded not only respect, but at length (when he was more maturely heard and listened to) admiration, awe, and at last dread and terror; which altogether must needs conspire to rid the world of a monster, whose more than human talents must be cut down to less than human measurement.

That Wi-jun-jon should be killed was decided in a secret council, but the method of killing a man so full of medicine required divine inspiration. An ordinary bullet would not kill such a great liar.

One of the braves obtained his dream and set off for the Fort at the mouth of the Yellowstone. There he obtained, by stealth (according to the injunction of his dream), the handle of an iron pot. He went into the woods and spent a whole day straightening and filing it to fit into the barrel of his gun. Then he returned to the Fort concealing the gun in his robes. He came behind Wi-jun-jon, while the latter was speaking to the Trader. He put the rifle to the back of Wi-jun-jon's head and pulled the trigger. Troops rushed in and seized the wizard-killer—carting him off to the Stockade.

Here is where I will end my tale of Wi-jun-jon in my book for his death shows the imprudence of actually telling all you know, but I will tell the tale to the end for you, W.O., so that I am relieved of its burden.

I was among the Minnetaree when I heard of the death of the "traveled Indian." I set forth, at once, by canoe. I had grown fond of Wi-jun-jon during the trip from St. Louis. I had often thought of him in his newfangled duds whistling "Yankee Doodle" and the "Washington Grand March." I arrived in his village three days after his corpse had been tightly wrapped and put on its platform—such is the Sioux tradition—corpses remain elevated until they have decomposed and are suitable for burial. There were many people and much silence and much looking at Wi-jun-jon's platform. I sought an audience with his brother or his squaw to pay my respects, but their grief was too great to permit visitors. I resolved to spend the night there and perhaps present the family with my sketches on the morrow.

I ate with Baptiste Vian, a Métis fur trader. We sat quietly telling each other our exploits and other lies. The campfires were ill-fed, and for the most part the Indians sat silently. A rattling sound came from Wi-jun-jon's sky grave and a medicine man walked from there to the center of the camp. He took a long draw on his pipe and exhaled a streamer of smoke in each of the cardinal directions, then to the zenith and the nadir. Someone else walked from the grave poles; although it was too dark to see his features. This person sat where the medicine man had stood, and for a long time there was total silence and a mood like those evoked in the volume of poetry recently published by Mr. Poe. Then the whisper began. A hoarse voice began to tell of the wonders of an Indian newspaper. I knew that the Cherokee Sequoyah had developed an alphabet for his people, and that four years ago there had indeed been a Cherokee newspaper. The voice continued, on how as he went down river to Mississippi the Talking Leaves was the only source of news. To learn of the world they had to learn Cherokee and that the paper was prospering under the editorship of Sequoyah's son Tsu-sa-

le-tah. The voice continued (as I continued to try and make out the speaker) on the wonder of a newspaper, how it unified and ordered the world by bringing away news from far places. At Vicksburg someone translated an issue for him. He heard how the Creek-American War had been ended by the treaty of Horseshoe Bend. Furthermore he had heard of the development of a calculating machine Babbage's Analytical Engine, which promised to speed up and perhaps transform the calculating business.

The whole of the night we listened to such whispers. Then just before the light of false dawn, the whisper rose and walked toward the grave poles. By this time it was completely dark, for the voice had insisted the campfires should burn out, and the moon was new. The medicine man censed the air and everyone fell asleep on the ground where they lay.

I awakened about noon. I hoped to discover who had brought about this ghastly imposture. I nudged Baptiste.

"Ben morning, Monsieur Cataline. What a night, eh?"

"You know the voices of these people, Ba'tiste. Who perpetrated this hoax?"

"Why do you say hoax, Monsieur Cataline? Did you not hear the Pi-jonse-ec-head's parle last night?"

"I heard the voice of someone pretending to be Pigeon's Egg Head, but what he told were lies. I can't imagine Menewa and Andrew Jackson sitting down for a treaty."

"Of course it is lie, Monsieur Cataline. It is a wonderful lie—a bon motte—that a dead man should lie that he is alive is the most sacree lie of all."

"But you don't think—"

"I tell, Monsieur Cataline. My father's people say they worship the God of truth and love so they lie and kill. My mother's people don't even have a word for lying. So I don't think too much. If I think in French I have to lie. If I think in Crow I cannot even have heard what I heard. And if I think in English I think of teaching a great man to whistle 'Yankee Doodle'." Baptiste wagged his head in disgust.

Baptiste returned to sleep. I prowled about the village. There were some scraps of winding cloth on the grave poles, but this could be a tribute to the thoroughness of the hoaxters. I hoped the hoaxters were not agents of the American Fur Company.

And I thought about the lies. This hope was a bad thing. I abandoned hope. When I studied the law I had hope. I dreamed of a kind of Eden, which we could return to. Once we got the facts right in a case we could return things to their original state. With enough facts we could go back to the garden. Then I practiced law and my hopes diminished. I defended petty thieves accused by pettier merchants. I tore apart families by settling wills written by men grown cruel with their familiarity with death. I helped fat smelly bankers deny the possibility of homesteads to honest men. And the judges I argued before were stupid lecherous men whose tiny knowledge of the law was only slightly greater than their capacity for fairness, and both of these qualities required a hand lens to observe. At first I thought these cases were freaks, sports, accidents; but as I came to know my fellow man I saw that these ugly creatures would never find their way to any paradise—that their mere presence would end any paradise they walked into.

I began to sketch their greedy faces. I have never told you—and perhaps there is imprudence in making such an admission to my publisher—that I have never received a day's instruction in art. I learned to sketch in the courtroom. From sketches to paintings and with these paintings of ugly venal men to the death of hope. I made a huge bonfire of the studies and I lit out for the prairies.

W.O., I do not think of the Red man as some sort of Nobel Savage. But they are of a different culture and that wall between us helps me from seeing their ugliness.

I wouldn't let a hoaxter create such lies. These people would have their hopes crushed soon enough. Soon the whites would come and they would be in a world they couldn't ever run from. I resolved to shoot the hoaxter so I traveled to the Fort to purchase a gun.

I have never needed a gun while traveling among these people. One night while staying with a Piegan chief I asked him if it was safe. And he said it was safe—there were no white men in two days ride.

Night came. Many were hungry for the village was over-full, but none were willing to miss out on the lying medicine. I shared out such supplies as I had brought with me and concealed my pistol beneath a blanket. The medicine created sacred space with six streamers of tobacco smoke. Then the shadowed one came. It was even darker this night for no campfires had been lit. I rested my hand on cold steel.

The voice began by telling of the submarine, a steel ship which could sink to the bottom of the sea, an invention of Mr. Fulton, the steamship man. It terrified many white men to see the depths with sparkling corals and fish big as tipis and under-water volcanoes—so Fulton had crewed his ship with Mohawks, who aren't afraid of anything. The Navy now had several of these ships each with a Mohawk crew with a Mohawk medicine man as chaplain, wearing a blue coat such as he had worn on his return. He had ridden in one of these vessels from the Potomac to Plymouth in England. He had been very frightened. Some of the Mohawks had put on strange diving suits and ventured forth to collect many-armed fishes. They had invited him to accompany them on their hunt, but he had refused—saying that he had never eaten anything with more than four legs and he was sure such meat would frighten his stomach. The trip to Plymouth lasted four days and upon their arrival some of the Mohawk braves had wanted to go ashore to carve a rock showing that they had come and that this land was now theirs, but he counseled against this—pointing out that white men have no sense of humor. So they merely observed the wooden hulls of the British fleet and returned back to Washington to report. During the trip back to Washington, he became brave enough to taste the eight-legged fish, which he said tasted just like passenger pigeon. But he did not brave the deep.

During this tale, which was much longer than I have recorded

it—for I was focusing on my stalking—I had managed to get quite close to the voice. I didn't want to kill anyone save for the hoaxter, so I needed point-blank range. I knew the tribe would apprehend me, but Indian justice is not swift and when morning revealed the imposture I would be set free. I could see the audience by the starlight but the voice was elusive. I circled and circled coming closer to the center. I came to the point where I must have been five feet away from him and still he wasn't clear to me. There was a cloud of uncertainty from which issued a voice. I very carefully took aim on what seemed to be the center of the cloud and a hunk of metal bashed down on my head. For a moment the pain sent comets of red white and yellow through the sky and I seemed to see a wrapped corpse before me, and then the ground came up.

When I came to everything was blurry. There was a gray blur like cloud and a brown blur roughly shaped like a man and a triangular blur light and dark. It smelled like mourning in a tipi.

"Eh bon Monsieur Cataline. You are not mort. I thought I hit you too hard."

"Ba'tiste. Why have you done this? I would've exposed him."

"We need this medicine, Monsr. Cataline. In the Beginning was the Lie. Think on this my frien'."

Everything swirled and I slept. When I opened my eyes again I saw the tipi plainly. Baptiste had left some brandy and pemmican—both of which have great restorative powers. If you ever wish to grow rich in London you should sell them to over indulgers of all kinds.

Baptiste looked in to see about me. Unlike the crystal clarity with which I saw things, he remained blurry and indistinct.

"The chiefs want to know if you will be good or if they need to tie you to a tree. What do you say?"

"Tell them I will be good. I won't draw a gun on their false prophet, but I would like to speak with them."

"They will not hear you. They no longer want old talk. They are looking for a new way."

"And what about you, Ba'tiste? Don't you make old talk?"

"I will not after today, Monsieur Cataline. I think this other world is better."

"You are a fool, Ba'tiste."

"Mebbe so, Monsieur Cataline."

I ventured from the tipi before nightfall. Many slept and those who moved about did so slowly, slowly. The peculiar effect, Baptiste's blow had wrought, continued in that I could focus on tipis and grave platforms, but found people indistinct.

Night came and I smelled the tobacco of the medicine man, but I could not make him out. The Voice seemed far away or as if underwater in the fabulous ship. It began to describe a world of hope whercin White men and Red men lived together—taking the best of each. The Red men and White men would dance their dances not only here, but on other worlds as well. And as the Voice described things more and more beautiful I began to weep. And I was caught up in my weeping and it was some time before I discovered that I was alone. I thought perhaps the family nearest me had moved away—closer to the center to hear the still voice. But I walked and then I ran from place to place where the people had been. The earth was still warm with their presence and sometimes as I turned I could hear the whispering in the wind—a word, a syllable—nothing more. Then I only heard the wind. Dawn found me alone. Even Baptiste was gone.

I climbed the grave platform of Pigeon's Egg Head. The corpse was there. So who or what had led the people away I do not know. My capacity for hope had become lame. Maybe the people are in the lying medicine world. Civilization took my hope away, but maybe they hadn't had that experience.

The wind blows and I know what the lame boy of Hamlin felt.

Yr obt. serv't.,

(signed) George Catlin

INNOCENTS ABROAD

Miss Daisy Henshawe was astonished at the hustle and bustle of San Francisco. And a great deal of San Francisco was astonished by Miss Daisy Henshawe. Despite the severe fashions of her day, despite her unpainted face, despite the way her mother had told her to walk and talk and hold herself, Daisy Henshawe was beautiful. Her mother hated her for this. Daisy had golden hair, brown eyes, and (if you were fortunate enough to be behind her on a windy day) beautifully turned ankles. It required little imagination to presume that the rest was beautifully turned as well.

Daisy was nineteen. She had never spoken without first being spoken to. Since the ending of her schooling at age twelve, she had never been in public without her mother. And she had never, ever, been out of the city of Jamestown.

And now her father was sending her and her mother to Paris to see that wondrous new structure the Eiffel Tower.

You could hear the winds in the sails for miles. Daisy felt that she would grow faint from excitement as the carriage made its way to the docks. She had stopped pointing out sights to Mother. Mother had been to San Francisco before. And Father merely looked worried.

All of Mrs. Gloria Henshawe's life she had wanted to go to Paris. Her father promised Paris if he could just find that claim. He always had a hunch. Just a little bit too late. Gloria never got out of California during her prime. Her father did, of course. Ran up to Alaska and died and Gloria married the first man

who came along. An undertaker and coroner. Marriage seemed preferable to starvation. In te long years since she questioned her choice. Questioned her choice when he would come to her drunk and smelling of corpses, or when a hush would come over a crowd when she walked in. In the early days she had had to wash the dead while John built coffins. Thank God Daisy took over that job when she was done with schooling. John was prosperous now. He could've afforded help, but he stuck with Daisy. He's only sending us to Paris as a gesture—to show everyone that he can rake in the money like any of the evil old men who run Jamestown. In any event, Gloria Henshawe was going to Paris without her youth or her beauty. What was the purpose of Paris without youth or beauty?

The hansom stopped and John Henshawe and the driver began hustling baggage to the tars. John wasn't even going to go aboard with his wife and daughter. He might weaken in his reserve—call off the plan set in motion months before. This hurt in two vital areas: the pocket book and the heart. He hated to see his daughter go to Paris. He couldn't imagine her returning innocent. He pecked his daughter and wife on the cheek. The cab began climbing away from San Francisco Bay.

* * * * * * *

The Judge invited Henshawe to his poker game.

"You're looking right prosperous these days, Henshawe, seems only right we get a chance to fleece a little of that prosperity."

"I'm a hard man to fleece, Judge." Inside, his heart was pounding with pride. He had bathed twice today—as he had every day since his return from Frisco—to completely wash away the smell of dead men.

There were four men at the table (not counting Henshawe): Judge Sullivan Vian, whose presence upped sales of hemp rope considerably; Ralph Whelan, whose legal practice specialized in claim-jumping and will-breaking; Clem Larapallieur,

who supplied laudanum and cannabis extract for all the town's aches and pains; and Clovis Durham, whose bank absorbed the miners' gold dust as surely as a black hole sucks in cosmic debris. Only the Judge was important. The Judge had started them all in their orbits and kept them there.

John Henshawe saw that the cards were greasy and spotted. Their patterns would be easy enough to learn—if you wanted to win the cash on the table. As a matter of fact, John expected to be taken in his first game. The red headed barmaid in the green satin teddy put a double bourbon by him. The Judge passed the cards to Whelan and Whelan cut.

The Judge said, "Understand your fillies are doing a tiny bit of the grand tour. I ain't seen no rush of corpses at your mortuary."

It was a mediocre hand. John took two cards. Full house.

John said, "It's always seemed this way to me, Judge. If there ain't enough business you got to make some."

"Now son, I won't have you killing folks 'ceptin' greasers and niggers what don't count."

"No I just make use of what I got."

The Judge's full house beat John's.

"A couple of months ago, Chu Chi died from smokin' too much hop. You may all remember."

They all remembered, especially Clem, who had run the Chinese hop concession out of town to pick up their customers. Clem had sold the fatal cake to Chu.

"Daisy washed him up and I collected eighty dollars from the county for burying him. Then I dug him up and cut off his queue and twisted some feathers in his heathen hair. I took off his clothes and pressed a tommyhawk in his hand—then I dropped the corpse out by Frijoles Creek."

Ralph interrupts. "I remember. Somebody brought the corpse to town and there was an inquest. They had to determine what tribe it was and how he died and where he should be buried."

"That's right. I got three hundred dollars for that one. The court ordered me to send the corpse to the Digger settlement

to the North, but since I knew it weren't no Indian I just kept him. The sun had bleached him out considerable by then. I went down to Mrs. Murphy's boarding house. She always keeps the bags of tenants that skip out. I bought the bag of that Italian fellow that came through a year ago. Then I dressed the corpse up Italian style. I rode him out to the Phelan mine and I let him down on the well chain. Somebody pulled him up the next day looking for a drink of water and naturally there was an inquest. We decided that he was a European visitor who had met his death by misadventure *viz* falling into the Phelan well. I got ninety dollars from the county for the coroner's court and then I passed the hat around to take up for a decent burial, on account of he was a white man, and I got another thirty. Well I put up a stone and kept him in my back room. He was tolerable ripe by then so I decided to skelatize him. I put him in a barrel of quicklime. About that time a Mormon party passed through— European Mormons on their way to Utah via San Francisco. I went by the hotel and pulled off one of their packing labels. I put the label on my barrel and toted the barrel to the stage depot. Well none of the Mormons loaded up the barrel since it weren't theirs. In a week the stage manager pried open the barrel and I was sent for. Well there was a big inquest on account of it looking like murder."

The Judge said, "I even had to extradite one of those Mormons and hang him for it."

"So I got two hundred dollars for the skeleton and fifty dollars for burying the Mormon and another fifty from his family for shipping him back to Salt Lake."

"You certainly got a lot of mileage from one body," said Ralph.

"I ain't finished my story. When I buried Joe MacKenzie his family paid me off with the rights to Split Pine Mine. Now the Split Pine weren't much 'count 'cause it had collapsed. So I took the skeleton apart and tossed some of the bones down what was left of the shaft. I got a pick and tapped the skull right here and then I put the skull on the lip of the shaft. Next day I ordered

the county work force to excavate the mine on account of the skeleton, which was clear evidence of murder. They dug and dug and never found all the bones. So I held an inquest on what they did find—some poor miner—no doubt a slain partner of the late Joe MacKenzie. Eighty dollars for the inquest and I had a working mine. I sent my family to Paris on that one corpse and I ain't finished with it yet."

Clem dealt the tenth hand of the evening and John drew three aces.

* * * * * * *

Chu Chi woke. The last of the poppies had been blown away. It was his longest and best trip. Truly Clem Larapallieur sold good opium. He must work hard to buy some more. He had dreamt the most fantastic things. Chu Chi stood and his head fell off. This was most distressing even to a calm-tempered man like Chu Chi. He knelt in the darkness to feel for his head. His skeletal fingers passed through the empty eye sockets.

So, some of the things he had dreamt were true.

He fit his skull back in place. Someone had knocked a hole in it. Henshawe, he remembered Henshawe and his nagging wife and beautiful daughter. He could sense the objects of Henshawe's small back room: bathtub, winches, slab, saws. But he could not see them. He decided that if his current state continued he would research the phenomenology of perception. Also: philosophy, theology, and medical theory of death.

Chu Chi walked into the funeral parlor. Two miners, dead from tuberculosis, lay in their respective caskets. Chu Chi felt no communion with them. Only then did it occur to him that his might be a solitary state. That he could not play fan-tan or mah-jongg with the dead. There were no dead to share a pipe with.

Henshawe's greatcoat fit him—he might be able to pass for a scarecrow at a great distance. He lifted the latch and strolled into the California night.

* * * * * * *

The four men who ran Jamestown were buying John Henshawe's story. They thought it was all his doing—the scheming of his fine mind. They didn't know that Gloria had thought up the schemes, nagged him into doing them. They didn't even know that he was afraid of the dead men—haunted by superstitions that most morticians bury with their first body. He didn't need Gloria. He'd come to this poker game without Gloria. He took a swig of bourbon. He would show them.

"I've got the skeleton back in my shop right now. Tomorrow I'll hang some green goggles on his eyes and some leather straps on his chest. Then I'll take him down to Dead Man's Gulch and throw the parts in a Balm-of-Gilead tree. I'll hang some silk from Daisy's old bloomers on the thorns."

"What the hell's that supposed to be?"

"An aerialist. A balloon rider fell to earth."

They marveled at his invention. They drank. He lost more. He doesn't need Gloria. Just Daisy to wash to corpses.

The gold pieces were piling up in front of Clem Larapallieur. The five men had killed a fifth.

"Well, Clem, looks like you cleaned us out tonight."

"Aw, Judge, you'll get a chance to get it back. I'll see all of you in the morning when you come by for a hangover cure. Cures are on the house." Clem swept his gold into a small cotton bag, which he placed inside his pants. The reassuring coldness of the gold steadied his drunken walk across the dark street.

LARAPALLIEUR
DRUGS & SUNDRIES

He went behind the counter. He was mixing up his hangover cure tonight. He dropped simple salts in a large glass, added water, and watched the foam. He was about to drink the concoction when he heard a scratching at his door. Perhaps one of his

Chinese clients had crawled here in the throes of hop sickness. Perhaps it was Mrs. Murphy's cat. In either case it shouldn't be at the front door. He pulled his revolver. He threw open the door. No cat. Something white. A skeletal left arm. Maybe this was that drunken coroner's idea of a joke. He kicked the thing into the street.

The hangover remedy seemed a trifle bitter. He was halfway up the stairs when the spasms hit. First his gut then in hot painful waves through his body. He lost his grip and fell backwards. Just before the strychnine finished him he saw the one-armed skeleton of Chu Chi.

* * * * * * *

Chu Chi ventured into the deserted street to retrieve his lost arm. He knew he needed better covering if he was to pass in the world of men.

Even for a trapper like Chu Chi removing the skin of the druggist was not easy. It wasn't as tough as animal hide nor did the drugstore stock any adequate fleshing knives. So the skin broke and tore and broke. Getting into the thing was even more difficult. Chu removed his head to watch. He stuffed his body with cotton and charcoal. Then he stitched up the rents with fishing line. The druggist's clothes covered most of the stitching, and with the druggist's gold he could buy perfect clothes. The face hung slack on the skull. The new eyes barely functioned. Chu Chi found a pair of smoked glasses. With his eyes shielded he could get by with object-sense.

* * * * * * *

It was the first time Gloria Henshawe had been alone with her daughter. Truly alone away from John's interference. Daisy, my dear, there is something I must tell you. The reason we always

keep you at home is that you are, well, plain. In fact Daisy you are ugly. You're a great disappointment to your father and me.

It was an eight-week voyage from San Francisco to France. They enjoyed excellent weather rounding South America. By the time of their arrival, Daisy couldn't look any man in the face. Even a priest.

* * * * * * *

Loud knocking broke John Henshawe's sleep. Nobody needs a coroner quickly. His trade is one of the few where the clients just lie there. He put his smoking jacket on. There was a Mexican at the door, his face hid by a large sombrero.

"I found a corpse on the road, senor. I have never seen anything like it."

"I'll get a lantern."

A skinless, eyeless body lay on the blood-soaked wagon bed.

"I do not think you will make much money from this corpse, senor." The figure had removed his sombrero. John saw himself reflected in the dark glasses. John made to throw the lantern, but Chu Chi caught his arm. The lantern fell into the wagon and shattered—scaring the horse and providing a bright, mobile funeral pyre for Clem Larapallieur. Chu Chi pulled the small knife he had used to skin the druggist. In the scuffle the knife found John's chest twice.

* * * * * * *

The aesthetic debate over the Eiffel Tower still raged. The introduction of glass-cage Otis elevators provided an excuse to visit the tower. After all the top of the tower was the one place you could see Paris without having your view spoiled by Monsieur Eiffel. The Henshawes came every day. Gloria wanted to absorb this view. If she could release a little bit of the view into her system every day, she might be able to survive Jamestown. Daisy watched the heights. If she could get her

courage up, she would jump.

"Monsieur, are you blind?"

"Yes."

"So why do you want to ride to the top of the tower?"

"So I can smell Paris from a great height."

Everyone laughed. After all Americans are known for their eccentricities. The blind man walked toward two of his fellow countrymen—or perhaps countrywomen.

Moments later a screaming woman fell from the tower. Daisy and Chu Chi were already in the down elevator, arm-in-arm.

HALF-DIME ADVENTURE

I'd found me a pan with no holes in it. I'd already plucked the chicken. I washed the pan in the creek scouring it out with sand. I made a little fire and hotted up the pan. I put pieces of the chicken in. Sizzle, sizzle. Pour in a little water. I would make a mulligan that the yeggs—a yegg is a professional criminal—and the bindle stiffs would remember till their dying days. They'd cough out pieces of their lungs in cold hobo jungles and say, "That was fine. That was sure some mulligan Tim Wilson cooked us the night before we stole the circus train. That was the best mulligan I had in my life."

"You can smell that chicken for a mile." It was Half Face Joe. A railroad cop pushed him off a speeding train deep in the Yukon. He fell into the rocks doing forty. He left half of his face there. He even has a hole on the ugly ruin of his head which you can stick your finger in and feel his brains. He charges a quarter for this entertainment. I only had the stomach to do it once and it was cold in there. Cold like the Yukon snows. I told Half Face he'd better hope for Heaven because his brains would melt in the other place. He carried a sack of vegetables.

"You buy those things, Half Face?"

"I jes' stuck my head in the store and they gimme those things."

We sorted out the rotted from the clean and I cut up the clean. Carrots. Turnips. Celery. Tomatoes. This will be a superior mulligan. Half Face carried the rotten things off. I suspect he ate 'em. He's none too cleanly. It was boiling a little too hard

and I tossed a little dirt on the fire.

Moses Donelly walked up. He kept body and soul together by DDing. Being a Deaf and Dumb man. He'd go to a pharmacy and buy some lavender cologne, then he'd soak several envelopes with it. Then he'd go door to door with a card, "I am Deaf and Dumb from birth. I need money to go to my cousin's funeral in Laramie. Would you buy a packet of lavender from me?" Sometimes he'd run into a real dummy who made with the hands. Moses would sign back. 'Course Moses' signs were pure bunkem. The dummy would know it but everybody would think, "There's two dummies talkin' to one another. Ain't it a miracle? God's in His Heaven and everybody's happy."

Moses parted the grass in front of him and soon was standing by my mulligan.

"It'll be dark soon and this jungle will be full. I want to be sure you get this." He pulled out a Dr. White's four-bit mickey. I put it in my shirt pocket.

"Moses Donelly, you are a gentleman."

"I remember when you sprung me from the railroad jail in 'Frisco. If I can ever help you. Let me know. I'm your man."

"You can help me now by filling this coffee can with water and then by setting beside me for a spell."

Moses was back in a shake of a cow's tail. I poured the water into my mulligan. Poured and stirred. Poured and stirred.

Moses undid his bindle and handed me a can of pepper. I peppered my mulligan just so. There were other fires being lit in the jungle.

"Tim Wilson, you reckon we'll steal that circus?"

"I reckon we'll try. Some of us may get killed but that's the same as any day. Any day you wake up you may get killed. These jungles are full of ghosts."

Just as I said that a cool breeze began to blow through the jungle as though the dead hoboes and yeggs were raising to my call, which is just as well. I'd rather have ten hobo ghosts with me than one live citizen. Maybe some of those ghosts would take the bullets for us tonight. They don't stand nothing to lose,

if you think about it.

Parsimonious Pete was brewing coffee. It would be weak coffee brewed from grounds that had already had three chances to swim. Nobody needed money as bad as Parsimonious. If he couldn't talk you out of it, it would just sort of gravitate to him. I once saw him pick up a dime by just touching it with his elbow. He was magnetic for silver. He'd probably talk some greenhorn into buying his coffee tonight. If anybody ever found out where he hid his money they'd crack his ugly mug. It'd be easier to find out what grows on the dark side of the moon.

Someone got a pot to boil clothes and all the bindle stiffs were gathering around. Moses took my spare outfit down. A fight started about then. One of the brass peddlers, a seller of "gold" jewelry, turned out to be lousy. Dead lice roiled in the laundry pot. I could hear some of the boys cursing Brass Bill. The curses would lead to shoves, shoves to a fight, and a fight to somebody getting killed. That would queer the whole business. All the hoboes would leave the jungle as soon as somebody got killed (even if they just got drunk and fell in the fire). I hoped Preachin' Ivy would show up. This whole caper was his idea and he could settle a crowd the way an egg can settle coffee grounds.

Moses came back with my clothes. "They're raisin' a fight. I didn't want to put these in the pot because someone's sure to turn the pot over."

Sure enough just as he said those words there was a great whoosh of steam. Somebody pushed Brass Bill down in the mud and embers. He screamed as he was getting scalded so somebody tapped his head with a brick. I reckoned he was done for because I heard them dividing up his loot—even his 99¢ a dozen brass rings that he dropped for a dollar or more. He shouldn't have come into the jungle lousy.

"You know, Tim Wilson, it's a mean world."

"Compared to what, Moses? Compared to what?"

Night came and about half the camp left on account of Brass Bill. Ivy still hadn't showed. He was supposed to be in town

getting rods. If he didn't come in an hour or so we'd head out figuring the town bulls had jailed him. I poured my mulligan into cups and cans and everybody agreed that it was the best mulligan anybody had had for quite some time. Some of the boys were pulling out their mickeys, but I didn't drink none because I knew Ivy wouldn't hand out any rods to drunk men.

A stool pigeon moon came up. Half Face suggested we bury Brass Bill or at least drag him away from the jungle. We got up a burial party and they drug him off to cover him with leaves.

"Where the hell is everybody?" Preachin' Ivy carried a crate under his right arm. He walked up to the fire and helped himself to my mulligan. "Ain't nobody here."

"Brass Bill got himself killed and everybody lit out."

"How many are left?"

"Ten, counting you and me."

Ivy thought awhile. "We can still have a damn good time with ten men. We'll just take the last eight cars."

He opened his case. He gave a gun to Moses and me, one to Parsimonious Pete and Half Face and kept one for himself.

"I bought these from Judge Cooley so ditch 'em if you get caught. Judge Cooley told me he'd hang anybody who showed up with his guns."

The burial party made its way back singing a low, mournful tune. As soon as they saw Ivy they shut up. Ivy's thinking all the time—there's a fire inside his brain and sometimes you can see that fire through his pupils. Stops a man to see that fire 'cause he always realizes he's in the presence of a man who is a little quicker than he is.

"The train will be along in two hours. Formeter's Circus will be in the last sixteen cars. We'll take the last eight. When the train starts up the big grade it'll slow down to two, three miles per hour. Parsimonious and Half Face will take the eighth car and unhook it. The cars will start rolling backwards. Everybody else will be on their cars by then. Our mulligan-maker and Moses will take the caboose. The railroad bull will be there with the circus strongman. Take 'em out. I'll take the fourth car. The

money box. I'll cut up the payroll ten ways. The cars will roll for twenty miles. We'll get the circus to put on a little show for us—then we'll let the cats loose as a little gift for John Law—then we'll ride off in ten separate directions on the horses the circus has so kindly provided for us. By the time they've sent a train to pick up the uncoupled cars we'll be forty miles away. Boys we'll go down in history."

There was some questions and some answers. Everybody speculated on what we might find. One man had seen a hootchy-kootchy dancer in a circus at St. Louis. He picked up a rag and danced round the fire to show us what kind of gyrations to expect. Another had seen a talking dog.

Stumps Magee asked that if we came across a talking dog we should give it to him as a talking dog would be a great aid in his begging. We took a vote. A talking dog for Stumps.

A third man had had his fortune told. A gypsy woman had dealt the cards. You will travel the country whole and not die until very old.

Parsimonious Pete said, "You mean they'll be gypsies on this train? I don't like it. Gypsies can hex you bad."

"Oh I've got something stronger than gypsy curses," said the man who just told the story of his fortune, and he pulled from his vest pocket a wooden pig about two inches in length. "I've got this pig and when I'm getting shot at I say, 'Little pig, little pig don't let me get shot at 'cause if they get me who's gonna take care of you?' or if I'm in court I say, 'Little pig, little pig don't let me go to jail 'cause if I go to jail you'll go to jail too.'"

"Where'd you get the little pig?" Ivy asked.

"I found him in the hands of a dead hobo. He was the oldest 'bo I ever saw so I figure he's got to be lucky."

The man polished the pig and returned it to his pocket. I could see the fire in Ivy's eyes. He was thinking about that little pig.

Half Face Joe doused the fire. It was time to take our positions. As we walked to Dead Man's Hill, I thought I saw Half Face open his four-bit mickey and tip it into the hole in his head.

I swore that if I get out of this caper, I would stay among men that were fully alive.

We crouched behind bushes and trees. They were running two engines on the train, which was one too short for the grade. Most of the train was still on the valley floor when the engines labored past. Sixty cars would have to pass before the circus would've begun to pass. Moses was coughing heavy in the coal smoke.

He was still coughing when our time came. The train was going maybe four miles an hour—still strong enough to knock your wind out if you catch wrong. We all sprang out. Moses came from one side and I from the other. I knew they could hear him coughing so I pushed him ahead of me into the caboose. The railroad bull was up and firing. He sent two slugs into Moses and Moses wounded him in the shoulder. The strongman tried to squeeze himself between a side bench and the ceiling. Half Face and Parsimonious had uncoupled the car because suddenly we began rolling backwards. Moses and the bull went down. I put a bullet in the bull's neck and then I plugged the strongman in the chest—just above a leopard spot. I never saw a man so surprised to die. He stepped off the bench and raised his arms as though to yawn and then he fell on the card table busting it to flinders.

I checked out Moses. He was dead. I heard a shot from up the train.

We were gaining momentum. Moon-silvered trees blurred by. I went through Moses' pockets. Two five-dollar gold pieces and some silver. The strongman didn't have anything but a bar of some soft metal doctored up to look like steel. It was easy to twist around. I pocketed it—figured I could win a few bets. The guard had three paper dollars and a brass token for a drink at Sally O'Mara's in Denver.

I tossed the bodies of the guard and the strongman off the train. Then I realized that I'd tossed out the guard's gun as well. Your own dumbness always trips you up. We were in the valley now all scrub oak and tall grass. The train rolled on at about

twenty per and we were beginning to slow. I lay Moses out on a bench. His eyes jerked open and I thought he might be alive so I talked with him a spell.

"Sorry that cough killed you. A cough's a terrible thing. My mother died of a cough. She kept coughin' and coughin' and my dad got her some capsules. Four grains quinine and one sixth a grain morphine. To be taken at bedtime. These didn't do a damn bit of good. She kept us up all night. Cough, cough, cough. Me just thirteen and going to read my Caesar everyday. *Omnia Gallia est divisa in partes tres.* And Dad a-laboring in his pharmacy. We just couldn't take it. The sleeplessness. Know what I mean?

Moses nodded or maybe the train just jiggled his corpse. I started to break off the legs of the card table. I'd get some linen from the back of the 'boose and soak it with coal oil. We'd need torches when we stopped.

"Poppa and I wore pretty thin. Everybody said that whole Wilson family weren't nothing but a pack of ghosts—no offense Moses—so Poppa compounded a new remedy. Five and one sixth grains of morphine. No quinine. Stopped Mother's cough right away. Same way sixty grain of lead stopped yours. If you see Mother tell her that I love her."

The train was down to two-three miles an hour. Parsimonious applied the hand brakes on the first car. Its wheels shot sparks into the frosty grass. Then the second threw his brakes, then the third, and so on up to me. The train shuddered to a stop. The air smelled of hot iron. An elephant trumpeted. I began lighting my torches.

Preachin' Ivy jumped off and shot his revolver in the air.

"I don't want nobody moving excepting my men. If anybody sticks his head out of a car. I'll blow it all the way to Dead Man's Hill."

I jumped off the caboose carrying all four torches blazing together. I handed one to the wooden pig man, who stood between the second and third cars, one to Ivy, one to the hootchy-kootch man, and one to Half Face.

"Moses didn't make it to the promised land."

"Well there's a little more for us. We'll have a moment of silence for Moses."

The elephant ruined the moment of silence by trumpeting again.

"Open up that damn car. Let's see that elephant. Maybe we can cut its tusks off for ivory."

The wooden pig man opened the ride door of the tall boxcar. Loose straw drifted out along with the smell of a hundred barnyards. Someone had already tusked the elephant. The elephant couldn't stand up all the way and sort of crawled forward. His big yellow eyes looked scared. He was looking for someone. It lurched out of the boxcar with a half-liquid motion. The pig man wasn't quick enough. The elephant's front foot smashed the pig man into the frozen ground. This really scared the elephant. He trotted a few yards away from the boxcar. Ivy shot the elephant's rear. It bellowed and went crashing off into the scrub oak.

"Damn murderin' elephant."

The pig man was a breathing bloody mess. There would be no getting up for him—no way to separate the flesh and the earth. Ivy walked over to him. The pig man nodded and Ivy let him have it through the heart. Then Ivy bent down and pulled the wooden pig from the dead man's vest and put it in his own shirt pocket. The elephant bellowed again.

"Can't ever have too much luck," Ivy said. "Let's open the other cars one by one and see what we've got."

"Let's divide the coin first," said Parsimonious Pete.

"Eight ways comes to seventy-five dollars apiece." Ivy started laying the gold and paper in neat piles. Counting out loud where everybody could see. Then we went forward one by one and claimed our share.

The first two cars held the horses. Half Face opened 'em up and peeked inside. Tack was there but the saddles must've been in the main train.

One of the bindle stiffs opened the third car. Eight chimpanzees came stirring out. Parsimonious started shooting, but

Ivy yelled at him to stop. Couldn't he see that they were doing no harm? The chimps made a four-three-one pyramid. Then they leapt off and tumbled and scrambled over the cars. One of them stole Parsimonious Pete's cap and was shot for his trouble. At the sound of renewed gunfire all the chimps jumped off the train and into the bushes. They vanished almost instantly but we heard their chatter as long as we were there.

Half Face went into the chimp car. There were eight little desks with eight little typewriters. Each of the chimps was turning out a five-cent novel. *Frank Reade and his Steam Man of the Plains, Frank Reade and his Steam Horse, Frank Reade and his Steam Team, Frank Reade Jr. and his Steam Wonder, Frank Reade Jr. and his Electric Boat, Frank Reade Jr. and his Wonderful Airship, Frank Reade Jr. and his Electric Velocipede.* In stacks of crates along one side was the whole of the Half-Dime Library. Nowhere was indication that the hard-working apes had received a penny for their labor. In fact, it wasn't clear to us whether the chimpanzees were the authors of these works or were merely typing them up from memory as a sort of entertainment. Parsimonious felt badly about shooting one as all yeggs and hoboes have a soft spot for literary men. Ivy told him not to take it so hard. It was a well-known fact that Mr. Edison was working on a device to produce half-dime novels automatically. Ivy had been to Menlo Park and had not only told us of the coming light bulb, but had stolen one to show us. If he could have only stolen a method of electrifying it—it would have been quite the novelty.

Parsimonious left the monkey car. He was outside, bawling his head off and looking for coin in the pig man's pockets.

The next car had held the lucre. Now the only thing of interest was a dead bearded lady and her pearl-handled six-shooter. The hootchy-kootch man asked Ivy if he could have the gun and Ivy said sure, why not? One of the other men said it must've been hard to shoot a woman and Ivy looked at him. I wouldn't've wanted to be on the receiving end of that look. It was a special Ivy look and there was death in it. Ivy said, "If it's got a beard

it ain't a woman."

I said, "Ivy, we've made real history. Even the James brothers never stole the train."

Ivy smiled and we all breathed easier. The moon was going down. Bloating near the horizon.

The next car had held the elephant. We collected Parsimonious, all covered in blood and tears. Half Face opened the sixth car. It held a tank and three cages. We each walked through the length of the car—passing the torches backwards so each man got a good look. It was early morning now and much colder so our breath and the breath of the animals steamed considerably. After this caper we would each ride off in different directions, but I knew in a few weeks we'd all be heading south.

In the tank: A half-man/half-fish swam in stagnant green water. It looked as though someone had hollowed out a thirty-pound albino catfish and stuffed a baby in it. The arms and legs were well-formed—just like a baby's—except covered in scales, each about the size of a dime. The head was large but fishlike. Its silver eyes were scaled over. I think it was blind, but it sensed our passage with its whiskers. Its little mouth worked. O. O. O.

In the first cage to the left: A two-headed black rooster beat its wings at us. It looked just like the chicken that I'd cut up for my mulligan (save for its having two heads). The left head had been fighting the right head. It had pecked out the closer of the right head's eyes. I think we all had to fight to keep our mulligan down—except for Half Face. He was the last one through. He couldn't stand to see this creature with two faces, when he had one half of one. He opened the cage and grabbed the rooster. He wrung both its necks in contrary directions, then he threw the bird out in the cold. It ran around in the frost with both heads trailing.

In the cage to the right: A rose bush bloomed. Each blossom was perfect and lime-green. The hootchy-kootch man reached into the cage to pluck a rose for his lapel. Two branches swished forward raking his hand with thorns. He gave a squawk and pulled his hand back. The branches resumed their normal posi-

tion. Blood dripped down into the terra cotta pot that housed the rose—enriching its soil.

In the second cage on the left: Only musky straw—a sexy-musky smell. Each man shuddered as they wondered what had been here—what kind of ghost the cage held. We were glad for the cold outside air.

We all regrouped outside. There was one unexplored car. We heard a train whistle from far away. That would be the train backing down Dead Man's Hill looking for its lost cars. More-n-likely it also meant John Law.

"Time to mount up, boys," said Ivy.

"Not me, boss," I said. "I'm going to see what's in that last car."

The train whistled again and the elephant trumpeted as though calling to its mate.

"Give me your gun then. I told Judge Cooley that I wouldn't let any of his guns fall into lawman's hands."

I hated to be without the gun, but I knew Ivy would take it if I didn't give it to him.

"Here."

"It's your own funeral, Tim Wilson."

The boys were mounting up—heading off in the direction Ivy pointed. I opened the last car. There was a long glass case in the middle of the car. In the case still as death lay a young red-haired woman. If it was a mannequin it was the most perfect mannequin I'd ever seen. She was dressed as a bride. She held a bridal bouquet of silk flowers—roses and daisies. A small plaque on the side of the case read, "The Amazing Sleeping Beaty. Miss Daisy Miller fell into a hypnotic trance in 1893 while watching a traveling mesmerist's act. Her parents have taken her to the most expensive doctors in Europe and America to no avail. What does this sleeping girl dream of? What sustains her in her five-year sleep? Will she ever awaken?"

I opened the case. I felt her cheek; to my surprise it was warm. I bent over and listened. I couldn't hear any breathing. I had to get all the details. I could live off this story the rest of

my life.

I took a long pull on my four-bit mickey to sweeten my mouth.

I kissed her. Full on the mouth.

Hell, what would you do?

She smiled a little, but she didn't awaken. I heard the train whistle—much closer this time. I left Miss Daisy Miller and ran to the horse cars. The horses were all gone, but there was a zebra gelding left. I put a bit in its mouth.

We rode east toward the rising sun.

BILLY HAUSER

The dusty streets of Amarillo lay still. Tired cowboys drank warm bourbon on the wide steps of the Amarillo Hotel. Vultures circled the city, their forms wavering in the thermals. Horses slept. Rosa told fortunes. A young man limped his way toward town walking on the railroad. He wore a costume new to the 1890's: white Stetson, blue satin shirt, black pants, white leather chaps, ivory-handled six-shooters. First Midnight Cowboy here on a September noon. Somewhere a harmonica played.

When he got a hundred yards from the station Rosa spotted him through her tent flap. She flipped over the thirteenth Trump, Death. The harmonica stopped. The sheriff looked up from his fortune at the young man. The young man tripped on a tie and fell in the boneless manner of infants. The sheriff rushed to the fallen. Rosa gathered her cards. She already had the dime.

The sheriff yelled and the bored cowpokes gathered round. "Get the doc" and somebody got the doc well into his mid-afternoon stupor. The doc had them carry the fancy pants to the lobby of the Amarillo Hotel. The doc splashed some whiskey on the innocent face and the young man rose. He said, "iwanttobeagunslingerlikemyfatherwas"

"Whoa, hold up there son."

"Iwanttobe agunslingerlike myfatherwas"

"Slower, boy, easy now. Have a whiskey."

And the kid looked at the whiskey as though it were something new, something unknown, and marvelous. He took the

shot glass and swallowed it all at a gulp. Then he coughed, spit, and danced 'til he'd brought the whiskey up in fine spray over the bystanders.

"He must be a Yankee."

"Must be a foreigner. Look at how he's dressed."

"He's from one of them airships like crashed at Aurora."

"Who are you son?"

"I want to be a gunslinger just like my father was." The kid smiled. He'd got it right.

"Gunslingin's no life for a boy," said the sheriff. "Where you from?"

"I want to be a gunslinger just like my father was I want."

"He's crazy from the heat."

The kid handed his shot glass to the bartender. He started to speak again—thought better of it and pulled out two letters. The sheriff pocketed them quick like.

The sheriff said, "Doc why don't you and me and the kid here mosey over to the jail and have a little talk."

The cowpokes hated the sheriff for hogging the mystery, but a man's gotta do what a man's gotta do. The harmonica started again.

The first letter was addressed to John Wesley Hardin. The sheriff hadn't worn that name in sixteen years. How had they found him? He felt like a stagehand suddenly illuminated in the spotlight. The faded creased letter read:

Dear John,

This here is my son. His father rode with you. I don't know his father's name, but I remember when you rode into town. You's the famous one. You's the one to train him for the life he's gonna lead. I'm returning to my family back East. Please take care of him. Raise him like his blood calls for.

God bless

It was unsigned.

The second letter was newer—written in an angled hand influenced by book letters. It was addressed to "Whom It May Concern":

Dear To Whom,

I've brought up little Billy here as my own child, but the needs of my ten other children are so pressing that I must abandon the little tyke and hope he finds happiness in an honest and honourable profession.

The sheriff sat on one side of Billy, the doc on the other. They tried rotation, they tried shouting, they tried tough cop and soft cop. All they ever got was "I want to be a gunslinger just like my father was."

They handed him pen and paper and he wrote:

Billy Hauser
Billy Hauser
Billy Hauser
Billy H

and they took the paper away.

When night came the sheriff lit a candle. Billy tried to pick the flame up. As Billy sucked his fingers, the sheriff reached a decision.

"Well, I guess we'll have to send him to the schoolmarm. The school year's starting and this boy needs learning." The sheriff wanted to show Miss Wyatt how well he handled anomalies.

* * * * * * *

It was 1897 and Greece and Turkey were at war over Crete, German troops occupied Kiaochow and Americans had been seeing mysterious airships for months. One had crashed in the city of Aurora, in Hidalgo County, Texas on April 17. A small nonhuman body and maps in "an unknown language" were

found. A U.S. Signal Corps officer pronounced the pilot "from Mars." For details, see the Dallas Morning News for April 19, 1897. Watch the skies and hear the wind blow.

* * * * * * *

Billy Hauser proved a super pupil. He stood taller than the other kids and handsomer too. Miss Wyatt found herself thinking thoughts unbecoming for a schoolmarm. He's only a child, she'd tell herself as she watched him knock the dust from the erasers.

Billy seemed torn between Miss Wyatt and ten-year-old Katherine McCleod. He'd sit at his tiny desk with his knees bent up to his chest and throw pieces of chalk at Kathy, a true sign of love if ever there was one.

One night Miss Wyatt crept into Rosa's tent.

"Miss Rosa, I need a love potion to bind my lover to me and shut out my rival."

Rosa handed her a vial filled with an oily green liquid.

"Pour some of this in his inkwell. He'll forget about Katherine McCleod. Thirty-five cents, please."

"How did you know Kathy was my rival?"

"Her red pigtails. Men see them and want to dip them into inkwells. In a few years a Viennese physician will explain these things."

* * * * * * *

The sheriff moseyed by the schoolhouse just as the moon was rising. Miss Wyatt marked papers by lantern light. He tapped on the window. She looked up with a start, which melted to disappointment.

"Say Miss Wyatt what if you and me went to the Founder's Day Dance?"

"No thank you, Sheriff. I just might have another gentleman calling." She turned and a cloud passed over the moon.

Billy's story came out in dribs and drabs as he gained a vocabulary. He'd been kept in a dark room which was neither hot nor cold. He was fed by "the man" a thin figure with a domino. The man beat him only once, for being too noisy. His only companions were two mops. When it came time to leave the man took off Billy's one-piece white garment and dressed him in the fancy duds. The man blindfolded Billy and led him up long long flights of stairs. Billy tripped fell and developed his limp. On the way up the man taught him the I-want-to-be sentence. The man put Billy on the tracks and gave him a shove. When Billy looked around the man was gone.

* * * * * * *

"I still say he came in one of those airships like crashed in Aurora."

* * * * * * *

The Methodist Women's Circle made him some proper clothes months later when his shiny suit fell into disrepair. The sheriff confiscated the firearms. Nothing was said of gun slinging.

One Saturday Billy and the other kids went to watch the buffalo hunters sell skins to the buyer from Chicago. Billy led the pack with his adult stride. He was several feet ahead when he turned down an alley. When the kids caught up they found Billy lying in the dirt bleeding profusely from the forehead. The doc came. Billy regained consciousness. "The Man" had done it. Billy'd turned into the alley and there was the domino and the glinting dagger.

The doc bandaged Billy's head. He told the sheriff that maybe Billy should learn to shoot.

Miss Wyatt had Billy stay after school almost every day. One day Kathy said, "You stole my man. You and that witch."

"I don't know what you mean, child."

"Well you watch out. I'm going to get thirty-five cents in my sock for Christmas and then we'll see."

Miss Wyatt went on with the lesson. Four times four is sixteen, but later in the week she sent a note home to all the parents urging them not to spoil their children during the Christmas holidays. Stocking gifts should be limited to, perhaps, an orange.

Because of his size Billy was chosen to cut down the school's Christmas tree. He rode out to Palo Duro Canyon with Mr. Lawton the head of the school board to select a not-too-twisted cedar. They were busily sawing the tree when Billy said he'd have to go to the bushes. He scrambled down the talus slope and Mr. Lawton heard a shot. Mr. Lawton ran to the prone Billy. Nothing moved but the vultures. The vultures always followed Billy.

"The Man" had struck again.

Miss Wyatt had to miss the Christmas dance. She stayed in the loft over the livery stable nursing Billy.

"The woman's a saint and a true Christian martyr."

"Don't the sheriff look sad without her."

In the early spring the sheriff began to teach Billy to shoot. They'd ride out of town find a flat rock to set up bottles and cans. Billy began as blind as a bat and a shaky shooter as well.

"You've got to be more calm. Be at one with your target. Take your time."

Bang.

Miss.

Bang.

"No, point the gun at the bottle. Just like pointing your finger at it. There's no need to hurry. Only the shots that connect count. Fire in your own time."

Bang. Shatter.

"You're learning."

He must really be Eric's boy.

* * * * * * *

A huge wall of gray black dust rose west of town. It poured toward the city. It stung and burned. Everyone took shelter. Except for Billy. Like the candle flame this was totally new. He watched the sun become a tarnished dime. He felt the dirt in his nostrils, between his teeth, pouring into his pants. He saw it flow and splash along burying his shiny boots. The buildings vanished. The sun vanished. It was almost night a superimposition of many tiny dust mote eclipses.

"The Man" stood before him.

Billy hadn't heard him and he couldn't see him too well, but he knew the smell. If he'd lived a few years later he might've identified ether. The ether and dust made his head swim. The Man came at him holding a large needle in his outstretched left hand. But Billy found his time. Just as the needle touched his left forearm, Billy fired.

They dug Billy out of the dust and listened to his story. "The Man" had vanished with the storm, but lots of blood marked his passing.

Billy ran a high fever for weeks. The sheriff came to see him every day. At first the sheriff was really interested in seeing Miss Wyatt, but the kid looked so—old. The sand had cut tiny age wrinkles in his face and the fever dimmed his eyes. The kid reminded the sheriff of the sheriff's father, who'd died of pneumonia. The sheriff remembered his father's last words, "Son, swear to me you'll never wear a lawman's badge." If Billy

Hauser lived, the sheriff would make him into the most noto-
rious gunslinger the West had ever known. The two of them
would ride out together. No one would be safe. And Miss Wyatt
could live at the hideout. He'd even picked the cave on the rim
of Palo Duro Canyon.

Kathy brought wildflowers everyday.

* * * * * * *

Billy got better. It was time to begin his training in earnest.
The sheriff walked to the livery stable. Moaning and thrashing
echoed from the loft. Had "The Man" attacked again? The
sheriff shinnied up the ladder only to see Billy and Miss Wyatt.

"Why you son of a bitch."

Billy didn't understand how anything that felt so good could
be bad. Miss Wyatt tried to explain to him as he hastily dressed
and put on his gun belt. He didn't understand the crimson blush
on her face either.

The sheriff stood outside the livery. He called Billy out.
Billy thought he was going to target practice. Completely calm.
The sheriff filled his hand with the notched six-shooter of his
gunfighter days. He stood in the corral facing the door of the
livery. He would shoot Billy the second Billy stepped into the
light. The sheriff's heart pounded. Rosa heard it and went out
to watch.

Miss Wyatt climbed down the ladder. Stop this thing. She
watched Billy approach the sunlit doorway.

Billy stepped into the light.

The sheriff fired. Too fast. The bullet sliced off a piece of the
lintel. Billy drew up his gun slow like. He found his time. He
fired.

Miss Wyatt learned a lesson in emotional physics. Friendship
(like gravity) may be a weak force, but it is ultimately binding.
She rushed past Billy to kneel by the sheriff as his red life
poured into the shit-strewn earth. Behind Billy in the darkness
of the livery, somebody applauded. Who could applaud such a

terrible act? Billy wheeled. The Man thrust an ether-soaked rag into Billy's face.

* * * * * * *

A month later: A young man in a silk-shiny sailor suit walks unsteadily along the Galveston dock. He barely makes it up the gangplank of a cotton boat. With unfocusing eyes he turns to the quartermaster and says, "I want to be a sailor like my father was."

And in a few days, The Man would once again diamond-etch another notch on his ether bottle.

SEVEN-FOUR PLANTING

I knew that the old farmhouse half a mile north of Hedley, Texas was haunted. The realtor even had me sign a disclaimer to the effect that "ghostly visitations would not be sufficient cause to nullify this agreement on the part of the buyer." Having two brothers who are New York lawyers, I added a writ, "providing that such visitation and manifestations do not cause injury to persons or property."

Twenty irrigated acres of red sandy loam—the kind of soil that pioneers would've given their eyeteeth for—it could grow anything. I would keep quite a little garden going in my retirement. My first evidence of the ghost came in the form of three yards of manure, delivered from a nearby feedlot. The bill was made out to Angela Thomas. I paid, reckoning to speak to Miz Angela about it the next day. Overnight the manure was worked into the soil, the tomato plants set out, and the bell peppers planted. A lazy man, I decided to forgo talking to Miz Angela. I caught a glimpse of her a few nights later by the thin glow of a new moon. She was planting the southmost five acres. I'd intended to let those lay fallow and hadn't bought any seed for them. But being how she'd done so much work for me already I couldn't begrudge her a garden spot of her own. Besides I didn't want to stir up any trouble; Miz Angela may have been dead these last fifteen years, but in the eyes of the town folk she was a Native and I was an Outsider. After the first spring rain her plants came up. I couldn't tell much about them save that they

were dicots. My beans tomatoes and peppers were doing good, and Miz Angela had sprayed a concoction on my okra that got rid of the rust. Curiosity led me to the nearest newspaper office (in the town of Amarillo about 80 miles northward). I checked out the obit of Angela Thomas. She had developed the Fireworks Assortment Zinnias for Burpee, the Silver Sparkler Dahlia for Park Bros., the Golden Fireburst Chrysanthemum for Lavilers. She had a BS from Texas A&M; MS, University of Cairo; Ph.D., MIT. She'd collected medals from the Imperial Chrysanthemum Society of Nippon, Kews Gardens, and a score of American gardening organizations. No wonder she could cure okra rust. By late June my garden was beginning to be productive and Angela's plants, which looked more than a little like foxgloves, were ready to burst into bloom. She passed by me one morning and sed, "I call them *hannabi* supreme."

Hannabi, Japanese for flower-fire. Fireworks. On the Fourth of July a few of my friends and Miz Angela and I sat on old lawn chairs and waited for the flowers to burst in sparkling lilac and gold streamers across the sky.

NIGHT OF A THOUSAND EYES

Ragan Haggard grimaced with disgust at the stench coming off of the Island of Dr. Death. Then a real grin filled his face. It wasn't really "the Island of Dr. Death." The real name of the island was Anderson Gulf Research center #10. He was just remembering *Iggy Twerp's Monster Theater* from growing up in Irvine, TX. There was something about the smell that keyed him into that memory. He hadn't expected that he would be on a supply boat delivering PCs to a experimental station. He didn't like the job, he suspected that Dr. Baptista was doing something medical, that required an island, something foul that needed isolation.

Ragan knew that there had been an outbreak of Ebola in Alice, Texas, and he fancied he heard primate calls as he neared the island. The ship's captain had had little to say, but it was clear that this tiny island in the Gulf of Mexico wasn't his idea of a fun port. Captain Sly had been listening to the radio all day. Ragan was sad at spending his birthday being tech support and away from his daughter, his girlfriend and his friends.

"I don't like the sound of the weather. A storm is due on the mainland, and we may have to sped the night. I'm hoping they can put you up, I'm not set up to be an innkeeper."

"What do they do on the island?"

"I don't know. They eat, I think. There are only four of them—Dr. Baptista, his daughter, a man named Pete—who is some kind of monkey doctor—and Dr. Baptista's assistant

Curtis. But I always bring them lots of food. I am surprised that don't all weigh 500 pounds."

"This Pete, you said he was a monkey doctor," probed Ragan still thinking of Ebola.

"I took him to the island a year ago. He talked about socialization patterns of baboons, I think. I am not a science guy, except for the Discovery channel sometimes back in Houston. None of them ever leave, none of them talk to me except for Curtis and Baptista. I don't like them." Then Captain Sly added hastily, "But I'm sure you will like them, you are a science guy."

"Well, I'm a delivery guy. See I got into customer support when my technical writing job played out, you know how it is—I've got a daughter in High School, she just dyed her hair purple."

"You know how to tie up a boat?"

They docked.

An immense man in a white suit was coming down a path to meet them, Ragan could see what looked like a small palisade fort in the jungle.

A shot rang out.

Ragan hit the deck.

"What the hell was that?" he asked.

The fat man was almost up to the boat. "It was my assistant killing rats. We've got quite a rat problem here. Are you the technical support man?"

Ragan stood up, embarrassed where his fantasies had taken him, "Well as much technical support as you can get. Can I get a hand unloading the equipment?"

"My man will be along in a moment. I am Dr. Baptista." He turned to address the Captain, "You did bring all the supplies I asked for?"

* * * * * * *

Later as Ragan finished taking the computer equipment out of its cases in the compound, Dr. Pete Ruchio came in. He was

a tall, thin twitchy guy that Ragan hated on sight. He reminded Ragan of an annoying High School counselor that had always been a little bit too intense on running other people's lives. Just as Dr. Ruchio began to introduce himself, a loud fight broke out in the compound yard, between Baptista and Captain Sly.

Baptista was yelling that they would have to leave, that it would interfere with the research if anyone stayed on the island for the night. Dr. Ruchio began loudly talking about the weather and sports and other drivel to try to drown out the ruckus.

Ragan said, "All of this equipment is pretty standard stuff, what have you been using for the last year."

"We had an accident, a fire that destroyed all of our computers about a month ago. We're having to start from scratch, that's why Dr. Baptista is so nervous."

"That sounds really rough. Is he playing with all his marbles?"

"What do you mean?"

"Well. We're in a fort. The Gulf of Mexico isn't exactly the pirate stronghold that is used to be."

"You might be wrong there. We were shook down by drug runners a few years ago. They thought that we had drugs or weapons or something. Dr. Baptista, Curtis and I built the palisade. It's probably just better for our nerves."

"What kind of research are you doing here anyway?" asked Ragan.

At that moment Baptista stormed into the room.

"Mr. Haggard," he said, "You will have to be our guest tonight, it seems. I hope you will not find this enforced hospitality too dull. Unfortunately, both Dr. Ruchio and myself are at a crucial stage in our research, so I hope Curtis can amuse you."

Ragan started to ask about Dr. Baptista's daughter, but decided that might send the wrong signal as though he was playing the part of the traveling salesman in the joke. So the island stank and was full of rats, and Ragan suspected nuts as well.

* * * * * * *

There were three buildings in the compound. Ragan had seen the partial interior of one, the lab, and as the sun set went to the smallest of the buildings, which served as Curtis' room. Curtis hobbled in from a busy day of rat killing, closing the gate of the stockade behind him. Curtis was thin, sun-burnt, and had about four days of stubble on his chin. He wore a stained cotton shirt, pants that were more khaki than any other color, and beaten-up boots. He packed two handguns, and as he neared his house, Ragan decided that showering was not among the man's hobbies.

Curtis managed a grim smile, "Hi. I'm Dan Curtis."

"Ragan Haggard."

"So you're trapped on Baptista's Island. Do you drink? Drinking's about the only entertainment unless I get something good on the shortwave. Come on into my building, I'll see about getting us some dinner."

"Won't we be eating with...."

"No. The doctors eat alone, engrossed in thoughts too deep for us lowly mortals."

Curtis was quiet during the preparing of the pork and beans, which with the tasty side dish of Saltine crackers proved to be the evening's fare.

Curtis made a pot of coffee afterward, the singularly most bitter, oily and vile coffee that Ragan had ever tasted. During small talk, they discovered that each of them belonged to the fraternity of divorced men, that great and brooding brotherhood that always has something to talk about amongst themselves.

Time went along a little more quickly after that. Ragan talked about his daughter in Austin, Curtis mentioned a son in Dodge City. They talked about the bad habits of their ex's.

"Yeah," said Curtis, "Marie was bad enough, but I could have been bit a lot worse. Dr. Baptista's daughter Kate was the worst shrew I ever met. I fell in love too, that was when it was just me and Dr. Baptista and Kate here. You always fall in love based on opportunity, you know. Thankfully Pete showed up, and she fixated on him. Everyday she gave him all kinds of grief, but she

was the only woman on the island."

"She still lives on the island, doesn't she?" asked Ragan, "I haven't seen her."

"Oh, she's around. If you're lucky you won't run into her. You don't see her much for the first couple of days after the supply ship docks."

The conversation wandered back to Ragan's life for a awhile, then weather on the Gulf, then dumb jokes.

It had grown quite dark. There was a rustling sound in the trees beyond the stockade, or perhaps the whirring of a large group of insects. Curtis seemed a little nervous, and broke out a bottle of rum to season his coffee. Ragan tried one cup figuring it would taste better. He had figured wrong.

There weren't many books in Curtis' cabin. Ragan had worked as a book buyer years ago, and always read the titles of any house he stopped at. Curtis's taste ran to techno-thrillers, Stephen King, three or four old pornographic titles and P. D. Ouspensky's *A New Model of the Universe*. Ragan had never been attracted to Gurdjieffian/Ouspenskian thinking, but a few of his friends in Austin had been quite taken with it.

"You much into this?" He asked Curtis tapping the green-colored trade paperback.

"Me? No, it was a big thing for Dr. Ruchio, part of his research, so he gave me a copy to 'educate' me. There was some good thinking in it though.'

Ragan didn't really care what the thinking was, but he figured making conversation was the only way to kill time.

"Such as?"

"Well the multiplicity of "I's". The argument that our natural state is one of being a lot of different people. Like you're waiting behind some woman in the grocery store. One 'I' wants her to just evaporate so you can get checked out, one 'I' wants to screw her, one 'I' wonders where she found orange juice in sale, one 'I' wonders what she thinks of you, one 'I' is already lighting the charcoal fire for the cook-out that night, one 'I' is off fighting with the boss from two days ago. There is no Ragan Haggard,

unless all the 'I's' are working from some common center. I think that pretty much describes the normal human state."

Ragan smiled at the truism, and then asked, "What did that have to do with Dr. Ruchio's research?"

"Dr. Ruchio took a different stab at it. Instead of trying to unify all the 'I's, why not get rid of those you don't like? Separate them and kill the bad parts. He had some luck with monkeys. He called it his taming process."

There was more coffee and more rum and more chit-chat, and then Curtis unfolded an army cot for Ragan to sleep on. Ragan's last thoughts before falling asleep were wishing that Curtis had an air-conditioner that worked for beans, and thinking that he would never fall asleep on such an uncomfortable cot.

* * * * * * *

He dreamed a little dream. He was back in his mom and dad's house with his brother Clyde, and they were watching *Iggy Twerp's Monster Theatre* and everything was in Black and White. Mom and Dad were gone and there was something bad outside the house, something very bad, and it was running and gnawing and trying to get in the house and it was very scary and very bad.

Suddenly they got in and they were a lot of dogs who were wearing costumes with big fangs and long shaggy tails and they were in black-and-white and they ran really fast, all these dogs and they were biting Clyde with their big teeth and then of one sank his teeth into Ragan's leg...

* * * * * * *

Curtis had grabbed Ragan's leg.

"Wake up, they've broken through, we've got to run."

"Who?" said Ragan confused and still half in his dream. A high shrill chorus filled the night. It was like the voices of children screaming, but very tiny children.

Curtis pushed him to the window. Some army of insects had gnawed its way under the wooden gate. They were big for bugs, maybe six to eight inches high, but it was hard to see in the dark. Ragan could see their eyes, thousands of eyes like stars in the night.

No, they weren't bugs. Rats maybe. But rats don't run on two legs.

They were swarming toward the laboratory. Their screams were in English.

They were screaming for Dr. Ruchio.

"Pete Ruchio! Pete Ruchio! It's all your fault."

Dr. Ruchio opened a window of the lab.

"I'm working on a solution, you got food today, what do you want? Go away. There's someone here. Someone that will see you like this."

Some of them were carrying little iron rods. They began tapping on the door.

"Go away!"

Curtis pulled him back from the window of the cabin.

"We've got to get you out of here, when they find you, they'll kill you. They don't like anyone seeing them the way they are."

"But what are they?"

"They are Dr. Baptista's daughter Kate. Dr. Pete Ruchio tried his process on her. He made a hundred of her, and they're all shrews. There was no good 'I'."

The door to the lab began to break, suddenly they were inside. There was gunfire. But guns don't quell the sea.

"Come," said Curtis.

Curtis and Ragan ran out of his cabin and straight for the fence. One of the little women grabbed Ragan's ankle and bit him. He flung her off, she yelled to her sisters, but the violence in the lab was too loud.

Curtis got the gate undone.

They ran into the night, toward Captain Sly.

A sudden burst of orangish light filigreed the vegetation. The lab was ablaze. Ragan thought of running back but the sound of

the Kate's tiny victory calls was too frightening.

They made the boat. Captain Sly could see the burning complex.

They cast off.

The captain dressed Ragan's leg.

"What the hell did that?"

"A rat," said Ragan.

"A shrew," said Curtis, "a killer shrew."

"I didn't know there were things like that on the island," said Captain Sly.

"More things than are dreamt of your philosophy, my friend," said Ragan.

(*for Howard Waldrop*)

COMMON SUPERSTITIONS

On his thirtieth birthday, Mike Jaynes experienced a Vision. It had been a disappointing birthday. His wife had been drafted into housekeeping for her bedridden sister. The secretary who arranged the office parties had transferred to Pubs last week— so no one at work said anything. His mother's card wasn't in the mailbox. Gout attacked his left big toe. The refrigerator coughed up smoke and died an hour after he came home.

Mike threw out most of the food (and the ex-margarine containers which held it). He hobbled down to the dumpster, heaved the plastic in; something gray and vile splashed out. He hobbled back up. He sprayed the shirt with Spray-N-Wash and wadded it in a corner. He took a six pack out of the warming refrigerator and four fresh peaches. He turned on the teevee. The cable was out. Natch. Mike had two choices. KAYS was rerunning a Lost In Space episode—the one where Dr. Smith demonstrates an Interstellar Vending Machine to Will despite the Robot's objections. Mike bit into the peach. KACC offered a short middle-aged woman explaining Sartre's Being and Nothingness. She said, "'Esse est percipi.' To be is to be seen. What does it mean to be seen?" [Mike opened a beer, threw a peach pit at the trash can, missed.] "Sartre offers us the wonderful example of the voyeur." [Mike switches over to KAYS.] "Warning! Warning! Alien life form approaching!" [Mike switches back.] "who is suddenly seen as he watches through the keyhole. Suddenly he is become thing-like, for the Other now has notions concerning his behavior. He is seen

as a voyeur. He has lost his freedom." [Mike switches.] "with Lee Press-On Nails" Mike turns the set off. He remembers his gout medicine and hobbles off to take twice the usual dosage to counteract the beer.

Mike drinks another beer, eats another peach and begins to sing the Birthday Song. Two more beers. Mike nestles into the couch and sleeps. Around midnight the television comes on.

"MIKE"

"What? Who's there?"

"IT IS I THE LORD"

Mike opens his eyes. A face of unsurpassing beauty and holiness fills the 19-inch Sony Trinitron. It is a human face but surpassing all in its perfection. After all it is the model. Mike wonders what it's advertising.

"I ADVERTISE NOTHING. I AM THAT I AM. I AM CALLING YOU TO BE MY PROPHET AND SPEAK TO THE CITY OF DALLAS."

Mike thought they'd got rid of the Draft. He says, "Dallas? Like in Texas?"

"DALLAS AND ITS METROPLEX. GRAPEVINE, IRVING, PLANO, DUNCANVILLE."

"O.K. I get the idea. Why?"

"THEY ARE IN GRAVE NEED. SO ARE MANY OF MAN'S CITIES BUT DALLAS HAS BEEN RATED MOST CREDIBLE BY MY RESEARCH TEAM. A MISSION STARTED THERE HAS GREATEST CHANCE OF SPREADING."

"Why me?"

"YOU HAVE TWO WEEKS PAID VACATION THAT YOU MUST TAKE BEFORE THE END OF THE FISCAL YEAR. YOUR WIFE WILL REMAIN IN ORLANDO AND THIS WILL SAVE YOU FROM A GREAT DEAL OF BOREDOM."

Mike remembers the double dose of medicine. That explains it. Mike relaxes.

"How are they supposed to repent?"

"DOESN'T MATTER. I'VE SENT TEACHERS TIME

AND TIME AGAIN. THEY HAVE MANY PATHS TO ME. SIMPLY TELL THEM TO REPENT."

"Oh. Why don't You send Your Son to do this?"

"SOFT DRINKS"

"?"

"MY RESEARCH DIVISION INDICATES THAT IF JESUS WERE TO APPEAR HE WOULD BE FORCED INTO MAKING A SERIES OF 'TASTE TESTS.'"

"Could you leave me a Sign You were here?"

The Face darkens, "SURE."

The teevee goes off.

Mike goes to bed.

Mike sleeps late. The next day is Saturday.

He walks into the front room for breakfast. He stops.

The teevee has changed into a teevee shape of lime jello. It quivers. Mike stands and watches it for a long time. He goes to the phone.

He arranges for a flight to Orlando.

* * * * * * *

The flight leaves Phoenix at 3:45. Mike buys one million dollars worth of flight insurance from the vending machine. He's wearing dark glasses. He slinks about. Half the security force of the airport is watching him. He figures he's safe if the video cameras don't focus on him. He avoids glancing at the monitors showing flight times. He ducks into a cafe. The salad of the day is bananas in lime Jell-O. Each of the green cubes seems to stare at him. He runs out nearly decking an orange-haired punker.

Mike waits at his gate sweating profusely despite the air conditioning. If he can get to Orlando to his wife to weekends of garage sailing he'll be safe. He'll beat this rap.

He begins to relax as the jet leaves the runway. He enjoys flying over the Rockies. Somewhere over New Mexico an engine conks out. The castor oil voice of the pilot assures everyone

not to worry. Everything's under control. The plane will make an unscheduled stop at the Dallas- Ft. Worth Air Terminal and passengers will de-plane during maintenance.

Mike needs to go to the john. Prayer begins everywhere about him. Sitting on the tiny seat Mike cries. Jean-Paul Sartre appears in the mirror and shrugs. Someone knocks on the door anxious for the pot. Mike recovers himself and returns to his seat.

In the Dallas terminal Mike makes his way to a pay phone. Someone presses a key in his hand. It's a locker key. Mike makes his way to the lockers. No. 1703 contains a suitcase. The suitcase holds a black friar's coat, car keys, registration, insurance, and parking receipt. All are in Mike's name.

Mike thinks the illusion of free will is wearing a little thin. He goes to the short-term parking lot and finds the car, a thirty-year-old red convertible in mint condition. He has trouble with the standard transmission and jerks his way to the toll booth where he pays $0.75. He declines a receipt and heads out to the highway.

He drives around Dallas and Irving and Hurst and Duncanville. He pulls into a Holiday Inn. Registers, finds his room, showers, puts on the monk's robes, drives out.

At a traffic light not far from Dealey Plaza, Mike spots some conspiracologists in deep debate. He yells, "Repent!" They look up stunned. The light changes. He drives on. He passes a gaggle of lawyers leaving a tall glass box. "Repent!" A stylish young black couple entering a Chinese restaurant. "Repent!" A group of kids on ten-speeds in University Heights. "Repent!" A man in a chicken suit in front of Eco-Taco. "Repent!"

He makes for the 1959 Texas State Fairgrounds site of Edward G. Ulmer's Beyond the Time Barrier, one of Mike's all-time favorite films. He makes four passes. "Repent!" "Repent!" "Repent!" "Repent!" He's getting good at it—really rolling his "R's" and really projecting.

Sun's going down. Mike returns to the Holiday Inn. He changes into his civvies and eats at Coco's. He returns to his

room, watches teevee, gets ice from the ice machine, decides to drink orange juice since he's on a mission of God.

He makes the ten o'clock news. To his surprise he isn't dismissed as a crackpot. The anchorman is solemn—asking "Who is this man?" "What is his message?" "What can we learn from him?" Drawings of the Mystery Monk are shown. He is tall, bearded, blue-eyed, authoritarian. Mike is short, dumpy, balding, and brown-eyed. This may be easier than he imagined. He leaves a wake-up call for 7:00.

The next day he hits church crowds. Baptist, Catholic, Quaker, Methodist, Lutheran, Orthodox, Reformed, Primitive, Southern, Scientist, Four Square, United, every flavor the phone book lists.

Monday it is public buildings. The Tarrant County Courthouse, the Dallas Civic Center, the Grapevine school board, a fire station in West Lake, the various Federal and State offices—F.B.I, D.O.E., D.H.R., E.P.A. He parks his convertible and shouts until people came to the windows. Some are surprised, some annoyed, some fearful, some angry.

Tuesday he choses orthodontists' offices. He'd worn braces and hated them. Perhaps the orthodontists, their staffs, and their patients don't need to repent more than anyone else—but certainly not any less.

By Wednesday, the Mystery Monk is featured on page one of the *Dallas Morniing News*. Police are said to be looking for him. Liquor and cigarette sales are at all-time lows. Wednesday night church attendance is predicted to reach new heights. Mike hits the shopping malls. For the first time his "Repent!" is greeted by "Amen!" He makes national news at 6:00.

Thursday he hits the two airports, the bus stations, the police stations, and the high schools.

Friday morning he makes four funerals, three weddings, an outdoor birthday party, and a company picnic. He drives back to the Holiday Inn for lunch. As he changes he decides he should be eating trail mix or something on account of his mission. He's already forgotten his attempt to flee to Orlando. In fact, he's

forgotten most of his past life. The past seldom leaves room for the present—let alone for the future. One of the benisons of working for the Lord is the ability to live in Present Time.

He drives to Ralph's All-Natural Food Bar. The parking lot is full so he parks behind the yellow brick building.

He eats a sandwich shaggy with sprouts and drinks a peach smoothie. After paying he lets one of the most satisfying belches he's let in years. Everyone in the food bar looks at him. He smiles nervously and leaves.

A group of punks are working on his car prying chrome off with crowbars. He charges them yelling, "Repent!"

"Repent yourself motherfucker!" A crowbar lands on his right shoulder. They are all over him. Feet to his groin, pulling his ears, spitting. He opens his mouth to yell and a red oil rag is stuffed in. His last sight is a crowbar heading for his nose.

* * * * * * *

He didn't know he could hurt so bad and still be alive. It's twilight. He's in a different part of town. Wallet and keys are gone. Mike stands up slowly and with great difficulty. He hears construction nearby. Some workers are putting up a condo. He staggers down the alley to them. He can't be heard over the sound of saws. He collapses again.

* * * * * * *

He wakes in the shadow of the completed building. It's a big one. He's grateful for the shadow at least—the Texas sun's a real killer. It is too painful to move. He will lay here until he dies.

Sunday comes and he crawls over to the dumpster and finds a half bottle of Gatorade and bits of sandwiches. He consumes these slowly in the shade and cries out to the Lord to save him.

On Monday the Lord sends a wrecking crew to demolish the condo. Mike moans for his lost shade, he coughs because of the dust, he groans at the loud tearing noises. A garbage truck

comes and Mike cries out to the men but they do not hear him. They empty the dumpster and drive away.

In the twilight Mike cries out to the Lord, saying, "Lord, let me die!"

"I HAVE A TREMENDOUS SENSE OF DEJA-VU ABOUT THIS"

"Lord, why have you taken the shadow of the condo? Lord, why have you taken the food of the dumpster?

"WHY DO YOU MOURN THE CONDO? THOU NEITHER INVESTED IN THE REAL ESTATE NOR WORKED ON ITS CONSTRUCTION"

"Lord, why hast Thou abandoned me?"

"I HAVE NOT. BEHOLD"

And Mike's mind is filled with visions of the great media coverage of the Repent! Movement.

"But my flesh has been broken."

"THEN I SHALL GIVE YOU NEW FLESH. CHOSE THAT YOU WOULD BE MADE OF."

Mike looks around. He finds a sliver of mirror from the ceiling of the wrecked condo.

"Of this."

"SO BE IT"

And Mike is given mirror-flesh that neither hungers nor thirsts nor feels pain. He walks back to his hotel and changes into his friar's robes. He walks to a teevee station and arranges for a press conference.

Everyone who looks at Mike sees their own face. Because of this Sign a press conference is soon arranged. The Mirror Monk will speak at Dealey Plaza near the Eternal Flame.

The next day the Mirror Monk walks to the bank of microphones. He says, "My brothers and sisters...."

A sniper's bullet strikes. Mike shatters into a thousand fragments.

Two days later a freak meteor hits downtown Dallas. The Seven Years of Bad Luck begins.

A RUNE FOR REBIRTH

Paul O'Donnel's one-man vendetta against certain Houston businessmen ended less than a month ago with his bloody death. His metamorphosis from a mild-mannered middle manager into an urban warrior seems to be a certain reversion to type. His grand-uncle John O'Donnel likewise had developed a homicidal mania in middle age under the influence of certain poetry or at least associating with certain artistic and scholarly groups. Conspiracy sites and paranoia-driven blogs have made much of the nature of his death and spread rumors about a statement found in his hotel room along with a priceless collection of weird literature from the 1930s. O'Donnel's surviving son and daughter have allowed us to post his final statement here as well as links to the Adventures In Crime and Space bookstore, where the O'Donnel collection is for sale in the hopes of ending undue speculation about the "O'Donnel curse."

The Statement of Paul O'Donnel

It began with the hope of money.

When my father died, there was a very small estate. His house, his car and a few thousand in CDs. I hadn't expected much. Frankly I had always done better than Dad at money. He had died suddenly, and I felt he had not taken care of everything that he meant to do. When I went to clean out the attic of Dad's home I found the boxed magazines, *Weird Tales, Startling Stories, Amazing Tales, Strange Tales, Fantasy Fiction Magazine, Tales*

of Wonder. All of these and titles yet more obscure had been the property of my father's uncle John O'Donnel. Great Uncle John was never talked about because he was a murderer. He had killed a man named Ketrick, because he said the guy was a snake.

Dad had mentioned Uncle John to me exactly twice. When I was twenty-one he told me that John had gone crazy in the summer of 1932. When I got my MBA he told me that "Crazy John" had left something for me that would be mine when he passed away. Dad wouldn't say what it was, and hinted that he might even destroy it. I guess these magazines were it. I never told my kids about granduncle John, of course the divorce took them away from me when they were eight and ten. I didn't know anything about pulp magazines—this could have been worth a fortune or be fodder for the recycling truck. I didn't know Jack Shit about magazines, but like all Americans I have the fantasy of finding that cache in the closet, that bundle in the basement that some nut with more than brains will make one a million-aire. I grabbed a few boxes at random and went to Austin's best SF bookstore, Adventures in Crime and Space.

"Since the coming of eBay used magazines are not as lucra-tive as they once were, but there are always collectors of the weird pulps especially *Weird Tales.* Three of the writers in particular draw top dollar: H.P. Lovecraft, our fellow Texan, Robert E. Howard, and Clark Ashton Smith. Your granduncle left you a nice chunk of change. Notice how well these have been cared for—the covers are still bright, the inside paper is white and staples are tight. What's this?"

This was a bundle of five magazines called *The Cloven Hoof.* Robert Clemants edited this small poetry magazine. It was illustrated by Austin Osman Spare and Hannes Bok

The book dealer was clearly impressed. "You have all five of them. There's a story about the fifth issue. It was destroyed or bought out of circulation or something. Can you give me a day or two to track down the story? The set may be very valuable."

Of course I was willing to give him a day or two. It was the

great American dream, inheriting money from someone you don't even know. It was better than the lottery. It might be my kids college fund. I drove to my small north Austin home full of warm sugar plums of cash...

I took my cases of magazines inside. I carefully looked though the yellowing pages of Weird Tales savoring the acid tang of the old paper. I checked out some stories by the bog three and found them full of gibberish like Cthulhu, Yog Sothoth, Tsathoggua, Gol-goroth, and the like. I frankly couldn't see the attraction. Then I stared at The *Cloven Hoof* No.5. It was smaller than the pulps, and had a glossy black and white cover. It clearly didn't belong with low-brow thrillers. I resolved not to open it. After all it was going to bring me big bucks. Besides it proclaimed itself a poetry magazine and I don't care for poetry.

My parents had always forbidden fantasy to me as I grew up. Such things they said were bad for the brain. I had had no Tolkien, no C. S. Lewis, played no Dungeons and Dragons, had certain video games taken from my possession. As I stared at the little magazine, with its subtitle of "A Journal of Fantastic Poetry." I wondered why my parents had erected such a barrier against the imagination. I wondered if it had anything to do with Uncle John. Had his brain simply rotted reading all this stuff and made him think Ketrick was a snake?

I knew it was a silly impulse, but I really wanted to read the magazine. I've never felt that way about a book before or since. I could actually feel an itch in my fingers to feel the paper under them. My eyes ached to see the ink. I found that I was holding my breath as I stared at the little magazine.

I opened it.

On page 24 was a fourteen line poem—if I remember my High School English they're called sonnets—by Granduncle John. It was called "A Rune for Rebirth." As I read the words I had the distinct impression of typing them on an old manual typewriter, a device I have never used. I had a hard time focusing on the meaning of the poem, but I had never done well in Language Arts.

My urge to read the magazine left as quickly as it had come. I changed into my pajamas and went to bed.

I found myself in a dream forest near twilight. Water dripped from mistletoe and moss, and mud squelched beneath my bare feet. I wore skins and had many scars. My body hurt because I was an old man of three decades. I carried a bow, a fairly crude affair, and a quarrel with half a dozen flint tipped arrows. My name was Aryara. I wasn't hunting for beasts.

I wasn't hunting for men. Not for the Picts or the Wolf People or the River People.

I was hunting for something like men. Something that had no right to look so human. Something that should not walk on two legs, but had gained the power to do so through black sorcery. I was hunting for the Serpent People. They came forth by night. The cloak of darkness hid some of their deformity and kept them from being slain on sight. They had two goals. They killed our men and they impregnated our women. They knew their bloodline belonged to another age, an age without animals that grew fur. They wanted to hide in our blood—hide beneath the red tide until the time was right to rise again. We were engaged in a long fight with them. The powers of light had called us into being to kill them off. We had hunted them out of the desert, the cold hills, and the great forest and now on the island where we erected great stones. They were almost gone, almost driven into the earth. But they were crafty. They knew magic. They had invented magic. And when human went to learn magic they were tainted.

I knew I would find some of them to slay this night. I had seen their serpent signs painted on stones and tree bark. The little people were preparing for a ceremony, a blood feast to the Moon. They would gather in a low place, a deep valley or around a well. There they would let blood fall deep into the earth. Then when the Moon vanished in fourteen days they would raid our villages trying to plant their seed. Only one child is enough for he may father ten and they one hundred and across time there could be more than we could count.

I smelled fire. The old men say the Serpent People stole fire from us when we came out of the cold desert. They stole fire and music. But we stole their secret, we learned how to be reborn.

I heard their drums and horns. They would be sacrificing. There. Ahead and to my left, the darkness grew darker still. The Children of the Night could call the darkness around them. I knew in the daytime a small valley law there. I notched an arrow and crept forward. The slope was slippery and I feared as I moved down into the magical dark that I might fall, tumbling onto their altar stone. I could smell the meat roasting and see the fire dim and darkly. Their figures swaying around it, their obscene pipes in their mouths. Two set drumming on each side of the altar stone and on the altar a deer gutted but not dead. Its entrails spread for the Serpent Mother. There were twelve of them altogether. If living was my only aim I would turn back. But I knew the secret. Die in the heat or battle and you will be reborn. If they killed me this night, I would kill them another night. I had sons. Into that line I would be born.

I took ten more steps forward. My eyes had adjusted to the magical dark. They were striking themselves with sharpened flints, cutting their scaly skins to let blood. Their sibilant hissing chorused with the ever faster, ever-louder drum beats. I came in low letting the vegetation hide me, and trusting that their reptilian ecstasy blinded them to my scent. I drew bead on one of the drummers and with a clean swift shot sent him to join the Serpent Mother. I got the second drummer and one of the chanters before they even realized I was mowing them down. They screamed as their ritual had ended with the drummers' death. They scanned the sides of the valley and I pressed myself behind and under a bush. I held myself still. I wanted to get a few more of them with arrows before having to engage hand to claw. One of them looked my way, and quickly I rose up and dispatched him. Then another met the same fate.

But then a pair spotted me, and before I could kill both of them, one sounded the alarm, and they began running toward me. I rose up and picked off a couple of them with arrow shots.

My arrows now exhausted I flung my bow away and drew my knife. Its flint edge would soon taste serpent blood.

It is the custom of the serpent people to look you in the eyes as you kill them or they kill you. This way you will know each other when you meet again. I rejoiced at their slit eyes looking at me as I drove my knife into their throats. One. Two Three. But there were still left and their claws tore at me from all sides. The two behind me were able to sink both teeth and claws into me. I could feel one of their claws cutting around my spine. I reached behind me and stabbed that foe in the eye, then brought my knife forward and slashed off the head of a fellow that was clawing at my right side. I made two hits on my front most foe, but I could feel weakness stealing over me. The wounds on my back and sides had been too deep. All I could do was trust in the great god Il-marinen to Remanifest me. I swung one last great swing, gutting one of the little people. My last feeling was the blood and guts dripping down my right arm as my knees sunk to the forest floor.

When I woke the next day, I was spent. Never in my thirty-eight years have I had a dream so vivid. My parents had always told me to disregard dreams. I remember once when I was four I had had a dream about large stone circles and drawing them with crayons. My Dad had taken my crayons away for a month and told me that "only little babies paid attention to their dreams and I didn't want to be a little baby did I?"

I did something that I had never done before. I called in sick to work. I wasn't really sick. I was just overcome with the idea that maybe somehow the dream was real.

I had never thought things like this in my life. My Dad always told me that he raised me to be a no-nonsense boy. I called Mr. Siros, the book dealer, but only got his answering machine.

I decided to go to Town Lake, the lovely green park in the center of Austin. Nobody from work would see me and a long walk by the sparkling blue waters of the Colorado would clear the weird thoughts from my head.

It was a beautiful February day as only a Central Texas

February can be. Redbuds were in bloom. Eighty degree winds chased the few puffy white clouds in the sky. I walked along the paths of crushed pink granite past the bronze statue of Stevie Ray Vaughan, thinking maybe my parents were right maybe fantasy was a bad thing when I saw them. There were four of them. In outward appearance they were two black guys, an Hispanic girl and a white guy. A little short for their ages, which I guessed to be about eighteen. They wore baby blue bandanas, baby blue jerseys, blue jeans black shoes. My urban sense said they were Crips showing their true-blue selves, but my dream sense said that they were Serpent People. The same ones I had killed in my dreams just hours before. They looked at me. They smiled and then they hissed and I ran to my car.

They didn't give chase, and when I got to my car I was furious with myself. Was I not a warrior of Il-marinen? I had fought and killed many more of these people than this small handful. What had I become in this rebirth that I lacked courage? I would return and fight.

I walked back to the statue and the Crips or Serpent People or whatever they were gone. I realized I was getting seriously loopy. I went home, and tried calling Mr. Siros again.

"I've got weird news for you." He said. Oh really I though there's a shocker. "The reason that issue number five of The Cloven Hoof is rare is that your granduncle bought up all the copies."

"Any idea why?"

"Your guess is as good as mine. But I am seriously interested in either buying your collection or selling it on consignment."

"Thanks. I'll get back you with really soon." As soon as I'm not hallucinating that I am involved in a Neolithic grudge match with Jurassic sorcerers.

I decided to try an experiment. No drugs had made me have my strange dreams or my little break down at the park. It certainly didn't come from the ooga-booga names I perused in Weird Tales. It had to come from granduncle John's sonnet. Now the sonnet did have two ooga-booga names: Bran Mak

Morn and L'mur-Kathulos. Maybe these names had some effect on the psyche. I tried whispering them over and over as I went to bed.

At first the experiment was dreadful. I couldn't fall asleep, and I was irritated with myself for trying something so silly. But after about fifteen long minutes of effort the names began to take on their own rhythm My body started to feel warm and melty, and some part of my being seemed to stretch out into the void. Seamlessly I was in a dream. This body was more like my waking self. It wore a suit. It sat in front of a manual typewriter in a cold New England flat. It/I was typing "A Rune for Rebirth" from notes on a sketch pad. It/I was my granduncle.

I said very slowly and deliberately, "I am mailing this tonight to my old friend Robert Clemants. If you know him it is probably because of his swashbuckling novels and not for his poems, which is a pity. If you read the poem you know you are me, and you know that we are Aryara and maybe you have found the dozen other names we have hunted the Serpent People under. I know that things are worse in your time. There are certain rays, certain sounds, certain chemicals that will let that which should not walk slither up the spiral staircase. In my time the Serpent People are few hiding among certain families from the British Islands. In your time they will be reborn everywhere. They will have their drums and their horns and the cities will know their mark. They will steal more than fire. Do not give in to the weakness of your age. Stop as many as you can."

The dream ended and I found myself still repeating the names Bran Mak Morn and L'mur-Kathulos. The dream was more vivid than the dream of the night before, but it still meant nothing. So my mind could come up with a reincarnation-fantasy involving a dead granduncle. If I belonged to another culture such dream were to be expected, but that didn't mean they were true. I would put fantasy aside and I would sell my magazines and that would be that. No nonsense.

The next morning as I stepped out of my house I saw that they had tagged my car. They had spray painted blue snakes up

and down the length of my silver PT Cruiser. There was also writing of a sort, a type of hieroglyphics that I recognized from my forest dream.

I walked back in my house and checked the Internet for the current phase of the Moon. It would be full tonight. They would make sacrifice. It seems like a good time to visit the Ten Percent Plus Cost Gun Shop....

This ends the statement of Paul O'Donnel. He had evidently written it at the beginning of his killing spree. It is unknown why he did not document the killings or provide us with more examples of his mania. It is widely supposed that he was killed in a gang shoot-out. In fact he met a more bizarre end. He was evidently attacked by rats whose bites covered his back, face and hands.

SABBATH OF THE ZEPPELINS

Malcolm MacKenzie was what we called a galvanized Yankee, which is to say that he had been a Confederate caught by the North then freed on the condition that he would soldier against the Indians on the Western frontier. That's as good an introduction as any. It tells you that he was a hard-luck case and that he was in his 50s during the Phantom Airship Flap of 1897. And being an ex-Confederate, when he met a being that was pretty near God—and found out that he was a black man—he was pretty broke up about it.

The flap itself had started during Thanksgiving Week 1896. According to an article in the *San Francisco Call*, an electrician named J. A. Heron had been contacted by airship pilots. They took him to a deserted field north of San Francisco and he performed repairs on their craft. As a reward for his labor he was taken on a 4,400-mile journey to the Hawaiian Islands. The trip took 34 hours. He described the vessel as resembling a great silver cigar, which caused many of us to take the cigars we were smoking out of our mouths and examine them closely. A week later the Call reported that Mr. Heron's wife reported that Mr. Heron had been in bed asleep during the supposed journey. We all laughed at our foolishness until Rosa, who tells the Tarot cards for a dime, said there might be more to that story than meets the eye. None of us asked her what she meant because she charged a nickel to answer questions. Hamlet MacKenzie may have asked her later. He was nickeling and diming his

daddy to death, but that comes in later. Instead we moved out onto the porch and watched the skies. We all wanted to see that airship. Who wouldn't want to be able to bring a cold breeze to the backs of his fellows around the campfire by saying, "I have seen strange shadows in the sky."?

Malcolm MacKenzie had no time for airship watching. His wife had up and died on him two years ago. His two daughters Jeffalina Davis MacKenzie and Roberta Elee MacKenzie were gettin' near marriageable age and the boys in the bunkhouse were gettin' a mite too sociable. And then there was his son Hamlet—who was named by his mother and thus avoided a Civil War handle—had he been born anywhere or anywhen else his curiosity and drive would have made him into a fine philosopher, scientist, or fictioneer. Hamlet spent handfuls of dimes with Rosa learning the arcane lore of the gypsy peoples—and much else besides. Hamlet had himself a personal telegraph station run out to the ranch. That's right, a personal station with wires run along the fence posts all the way from town. He spent hours getting and receiving message from other operators. He said he was a node in the worldnet but nobody rightly understood Hamlet. Most folks thought Hamlet was loco. In fact, we'd often debate it right on the porch of the Amarillo Hotel—was Hamlet loco?

The next sighting of the airship was by a Texan and therefore of unquestioned veracity. In the *Daily Texarkanian* April 25, 1897 Judge Lawrence A. Byrne reported that he had seen the airship at the McKinney bayou. The ship landed and is pilots showed him through. The judge explained "about the machinery being made out of aluminum and the gas to raise and lower the monster was pumped into an aluminum tank when the ship was to be raised and let out when the ship was to be lowered." Hamlet MacKenzie, who took damn near every paper in Texas, read the article to us hisself. And you can bet there was a lot of watching the sky that night.

Hamlet rode off to sample some of his sweetheart's larruping good pecan pie. Hamlet was a sweet lad, a late bloomer, no

doubt due to his mother's tender influence. He was between hay and grass—or as you might say, boyhood and manhood. He still had not put away boyish things like his telegraph and his sense of wonder—and many of us hoped he never did.

Meanwhile there was trouble on MacKenzie ranch. While Hamlet was off pirootin' with his sweetheart, four of Malcolm's best cows—all of 'em with calves—had come down with the staggers. Malcolm stayed up all night with them, nursing them—drilling holes in their horns and pouring in boiled milk.

One of his hired hands rode off the next morning—saying that if a herd gets the staggers it'll get dead. Might as well start looking for work now.

* * * * * * *

Cow carcasses swelling up in the sun. Bursting. Turkey buzzards and the little orange and yellow flowers of a Panhandle spring. Creek running low and Hamlet looking pale from so much time at his telegraph. He was very concerned about what the Turks were doing to the Armenians. Genocide was still a new word then.

Malcolm's arthritis began to act up and there seemed to always be bills waiting for him in town.

Hamlet rode into town on his sorrel gelding to pick up some bills, some salve for the cattle, and his copy of the *Argus-Leader* of Sioux Falls, South Dakota. Seems that two farmhands, Adolph Winkle and John Hulle, had signed affidavits stating that the airship had landed two miles outside of town to repair some electrical apparatus on board. The boys had talked to the occupants, who said they had flown over a hundred miles in thirty minutes and would "mail a report to the government when Cuba is declared free." He waited around mournfully like he was about to spend some money at Rosa's table, but thought better of it, and rode off.

His sweetheart, Emily Boadicea Jones, strolled by a tad later and asked if any of us had seen Hamlet. We told her he had just

rode off, and she looked near to tears. Hadn't seen him much lately, she said.

* * * * * * *

"It's like this, son—what with the cattle dying, I just can't afford to keep you in luxuries. I admire this worldnet concept you've thought up and I know you're vitally interested in the situations in Cuba and Armenia, but son you're gonna have to be like the rest of us and just wait on your news from word of mouth."

"Will I have to cut off my studies with Rosa, too?"

"Son, I promised your mother I'd take care of you. I don't know for the life of me why you hang around the old heathen with her terror cards and spells. It just ain't, it just ain't white, son. I'll let you have a dime a week and for the love of God don't tell me how you spend it."

* * * * * * *

We all heard of Hamlet's plight. He weren't the kind of man to keep his troubles to himself.

"If you ask me, that boy had been spending too much of his daddy's money. This is liable to make a man out of him," said Sam the barkeep, drawn to an easy consensus like iron filings to a magnet.

Hamlet didn't ever hear the remark because he was in the curtained off area with Rosa—that dimly lit chamber where the course of the future was made plain to you for a small fee. One of the boys walked over and put his ear to the filthy red satin drapes listening to their exchange, and manfully trying not to choke from the combined smells of stale patchouli and the fermenting brown spittle in the gaboons.

"... and that's the story, Rosa. Well, I have these two nickels."

"So you can ask two questions."

"Rosa, I've given you a passel full of nickels in the past, can't

I have a few freebies?"

"I've told you before, if you don't pay for it you won't have any respect for it. Mysteries may be cheap, but they ain't free."

"But I've got to know. I have to know things."

"You father has buried a coffee can full of silver dollars in the stall of his favorite horse."

"That's against emergency. So he can take care of his payroll."

"You live to know things. Would Faust have hesitated to steal it?"

"Who's Faust?"

"Do you want to pay for that question?"

"No."

After a beat he spoke again, sliding a nickel across the table.

"Rosa, this airship thing. What's the real key to what's going on here?"

"The real key is in the first sighting. Not in the man's experience but in what his wife said."

"What will bring me closest to the airship—where do I start?"

"The first step is obtaining a Sears and Roebuck catalog. Go, I can tell you no more."

As he rode back to the ranch he saw the telegraph company clipping his wire.

* * * * * * *

Hamlet's papers continued to come—and as he stopped riding into town daily—we took to reading them, then folding them up nicely. We noted some things about the airship.

* In Jasserand, Texas, it had brilliant lights, and the farmer who encountered the crew by night was told it ran on "condensed electricity."

* In Harrisburg, Arkansas, the airship had a gun capable of firing 63,000 times a minute. The crew told "Ex-Senator

Harris," when they awakened him at 1 A.M., that the ship was held aloft by anti-gravitation wire. They were planning to go to Armenia or Mars soon.

* In Holton, Michigan, the airship took an "honest citizen" for a ride, after which he talked of nothing but aerial navigation and the great revelry of the night.

* The airship was seen at night by many men. It was seen in Pine Lake, Michigan; Eldora, Iowa; Dallas, Texas; Waterloo, Iowa; Sisterville, Virginia. It was on its way to Greece, Cuba, Armenia, Mars, or New York. It had bright lights. It needed electrical repairs, water, beef, trout, bluestone, and a corkscrew. It was 200 feet long, 800 feet long, half a mile long.

And the occupants wore goggles, smoked glass or mirror shades.

* * * * * * *

Jeffalina Davis MacKenzie rode into town on a buckboard driven by Joseph Carpenter, foreman at the MacKenzie ranch. She bought two gingham dresses and spent the afternoon with her best friend, Emily Jones. They rode south as the sun began to set—whereas the ranch lay to the north. When Emily closed up her dress shop, she stopped by the Amarillo Hotel for a plate of black-eyed peas and ham hock. We questioned her. She said that Jeffalina had rode off with Joseph never to return. Did she know any particulars? Two things. One, Hamlet was stalking around the ranch with a wild look in his eye and his shirt done up wrong. Two, wherever she went to she was going to get a better name than Jeffalina.

* * * * * * *

A week went by without Hamlet showing up at all. The Sears catalog arrived in the mail, and we went over its contents with

a fine-tooth comb. We didn't find nothing. Maybe Rosa had just been spoofing. But that didn't seem like our Rosa. Many a man rubbed a nickel between his thumb and forefinger, but none of us asked. Rosa had learned her trade from the Python, skin-shedding oracle of Apollo. She knew the striptease of mystery. Show a little bit, but a very little bit, and leave them wanting more. All art, perhaps, comes down to the hootchy-kootchy dance of Salome. You could lose all your nickels trying to force the feather boa from her shoulder. So we didn't ask. We were grown men, mature men, men with families.

We needed our nickels.

The most spectacular sighting of the airship occurred in Vernon, Kansas. Mr. Alexander Hamilton, a well-established farmer, whose veracity was guaranteed by the sheriff, mayor, and other established citizens, revealed (in *The Farmers Advocate*) the dark doings of the airship. It passed over his farm late at night. "It was brilliantly lighted within, and everything was clearly visible." Occupied by six of the strangest beings he had ever seen, Mr. Hamilton could not understand their language. Their intent seemed clear enough. As the great craft whished over the farm, a three-year old heifer began to bawl. Mr. Hamilton ran to its aid and found a thick red cord about its neck. The cord was tangled in his barb wire and went on up to the brightly lit ship. He tried to free the terrified animal, but his barlow pen knife just skittered across the hard surface. The fence wire began to twang and pop from the posts. So Mr. Alexander Hamilton stepped over to it and cut the wire away from the red cord. At once the heifer began to rise in the air, and as the airship floated out of sight, it screamed and screamed in terror.

When we read this account, we grew cold in sickness and fear. Yet the sight of the cow rising (in our mind's eye) redoubled the curiosity. Someone said, Hamlet ought to know about this. Somebody else volunteered to take *The Farmers Advocate* and the Sears catalog out to Hamlet. There was an unspoken desire for all the things that came afterward. We wanted him to

do what he did—so we are just as guilty.

Silver dollars have a special rich sound when they fall on a wooden table—banging one against the other and the wood. The sight or the sound or the smell of money is always a powerful message. It's a strong enough message that it will cut through all others in a crowded, noisy room. All heads turn. But this sound was particularly poignant. We knew that Hamlet had dug up his father's savings. It would be awhile before old Malcolm knew, but we knew. And when that rich clang of money came from behind Rosa's curtains, Emily Jones put down her fork. She got real pale, because a lot of her future was in that money. She left the dining room, kind of drifted out, and was never the same afterward.

"Take it," Hamlet said.

We couldn't hear what followed, as though Rosa had used her witchcraft to put a wall of silence around her place. Well Hamlet had paid dearly for her information. After half an hour, Hamlet emerged from behind the drapes with an ashen expression and the Sears catalog under his arm. He got some paper from the desk clerk and straightaway wrote out an order. He left it with the clerk along with some money for its postage, and to pay for the item when it arrived.

We questioned the clerk after Hamlet's departure. The item would cost $2.30. Hamlet said it would be a small box.

We moved out onto the porch to whittle and watch the skies. Somebody opined that we were too excited by this thing—after all, there had been cigar-shaped balloons in Europe. True, everyone agreed (for we were a well-informed bunch), but those had been crude affairs. They didn't whish or swoop, they didn't have powerful searchlights or massive guns. When their inventors tried to fly them, it was by day in front of huge crowds. This mystery came forth by night. Someone—or something, remembering the words of Mr. Hamilton—had a vastly superior tech-

nology to our own.

* * * * * * *

"You spent all of my money—everything—on this? A two-ounce jar of thornapple salve?"

"It's more than a jar of thornapple salve, Dad, it's the key to the airship mystery."

"'It's the key to the airship mystery'," Malcolm mocked, "It's the key to my losing the ranch. It's the key to me being landless and poor in my old age. It's the key to losing every single thing your mother and I built. I thought there was some home in you, some glimmer of responsibility. You stole from your own father. You think I just planted that jar and money grew in it. Did your witch tell you that? But even worse, you stole it."

"I had to know and as soon as I know fully, I'll write a book about it and we'll have lots of money."

"Son, them starry notions ain't gonna put bread on the table, but that still don't address the question of being a thief. You're a thief and everybody knows it. A thief and a consorter with the dark-skinned gypsy witch. You've brought a blot to our name. I can't think of you as a MacKenzie no more. Take this."

Malcolm drew a wad of blue backs—Confederate money he carried for cigarette papers—and slapped it down on the kitchen table. "Take these, that's all you're worth to me. Put it in your saddle bag. I'll give you a horse and tack. Then ride the hell off my ranch. If I ever find out you're using the family name, I'll hunt you down and kill you."

Hamlet reached for the blue glass jar of thornapple salve, but Malcolm picked up a table knife.

Malcolm said, "I'll keep this. It was bought with my money. It's mine."

Hamlet saw something he had never seen—the terrible power of the father. He went to his room.

The boys were out fence mending, and Roberta had rode out to take them supper. Hamlet was alone in the big house with

his father, and he heard something he had never heard before. His father was sobbing, which was like a bone in his throat. Sometimes he caught words. "First Jeffalina and now him, what have I done wrong? I tried. I really tried, Maudie. I tried to be a good father." Hamlet's saddle bag was small so filling it up was easy. He'd had to leave behind his clippings and telegrams, browning paper assortments of anomalies and miracles, wars and rumors of wars. He left aside the chunk of meteorite and shells from a sea he'd never seen.

He went to say goodbye, but he saw tears on his father's face and in the presence of this mystery he was silent. He went out the back way, and all his father heard was the closing of the door.

With the falling of night he rode to Emily's. She rented the small house her parents used to own. She kept a few hens and had a garden. He knocked very softly.

We'll draw a veil over that scene. Protective loving feelings overcame judgment and we always thought of Emily as a used woman after that night.

Malcolm had been very still sitting in his chair—slumped over the kitchen table. Sobs had ceased to rock his body, but he was tired from the sobbing. Just tired and he ached. He rose his head up slowly, and saw that it was dark. Roberta should be back by now. He thought of going to her bedroom, kissing her brow. His one good child. But suddenly fear possessed him that she might not be there. That she might be out with the boys seduced to performing wild acts. He could believe any monstrous thing of his offspring now and he wasn't ready for the possible revelations that could come from opening that door.

He picked up the jar of salve. He could smell its strong medicine smell. He thought that he ought to throw it out. "For arthritis, rheumatism, gout, bursitis, chill blains, pains in the joints, male and female complaints, lack of energy. Good for man or beast." Ah, he thought, there is balm in Gilead.

He took off his shirt and wiped off his arms and upper body with a scrap of red towel that served as a kitchen rag. He opened

the jar and dipped three fingers into the snot-green, cold unguent. It was thick, jelly-like, but it spread like fire on his flesh. It found tiny cuts that he didn't know of, and made them shout out their presence. With numbing ice-heat it soothed sore muscles. It seemed to go into his lungs and out his nostrils like smoke. He could feel it in his blood and on the inside of his eye sockets. It had a rich alien smell—something like the sharp smell of a creosote bush after a rain, something like desert sage, something like the incense he had smelled once in a Catholic church in Vicksburg. He plopped down in the chair, his eyes closed, giving himself entirely to the alien scent. It was the only time in years, perhaps the only time since making love to Maudie, that he had given himself totally to sensation. He closed his eyes and breathed in, breathed out. Felt the heat. Breathed in, breathed out.

He must have slept a short time, before he heard the rustling in the grass. Somebody was out by the well. It couldn't be the boys, they were sleeping halfway across the ranch. Hamlet wouldn't have come back—he was honorable about some things—there was some of his pappy in him. Malcolm smiled in the dark realizing that he wasn't a total failure.

Rustle.

He lifted rather than pushed his chair back and got up real quiet. He went for his daddy's rifle over the fireplace. Just buckshot. He put his piece on too as he went to the door, in case he needed more than buckshot. He was glad he always oiled his door well when he opened it soundlessly.

There were three of them at the well. He didn't begrudge anybody water so he tilted his rifle skyward and walked toward them.

He said, "Howdy."

Instantly everything was brighter than day. A harsh white light that burned purple into his eyes. Malcolm tried to look up—to see where the light was coming from—and was momentarily blinded for his trouble. He could hear music and laughter above him. Wild and stirring music. One of the figures spoke

to him, a man. Could almost begin to see him through the thick light.

"We needed some water for our steam turbines, mister. Hope you don't mind." The man had a slightly buzzing voice as though his mouth wasn't shaped right.

"No, I—I don't mind at all."

"We can repay you for the water."

Malcolm had never thought of selling water to anybody in his whole life. Water was free. Heck, they could've gone another mile and got it from the creek. But if they wanted to pay. Someone laughed above. What the hell was going on here? Why did that light seem so thick?

Another figure spoke. A woman.

"We can repay you with a ride in the airship."

Now Hamlet had said something about that. Write a book, make a fortune. He would get Hamlet back and they would have it made. Maybe the boy wasn't crazy.

He asked, "Who are you people anyway?"

The man who spoke before answered, "Never mind my name—call it Smith. We just need to know if you'll take us up on our offer."

"Yeah. There's nothing I'd like better."

"Step aside."

Malcolm stepped out of the blinding light. There was a whir of machinery. Something was being let down. Sounds of chain and winch.

It looked like a giant's coal shuttle. The figures in goggles stepped into it, laying down their buckets of water. Malcolm climbed in. Inside the shaft of light he could see four stout chains that pyramided into one chain that began to lift the scuttle from the ground.

It rose a long time.

It stopped.

But the light was too intense to see anything.

"Try one of these." Some woman had approached the scuttle and handed Malcolm a pair of goggles. He put them on and the

pain stopped immediately and he could see.

The sides of the scuttle swung and the three he had ascended with picked up their buckets and headed across a vast hall. It was fashioned of a silver-gray metal like aluminum and its arched ceiling was covered in crystal chandeliers. Far more exotic than the twelve-crystal fob chandelier in his parlor. The chandeliers derived their flashing fiery rainbows from arc lamps and the crystal swung to and fro, vibrated by the movement of the airship and from the great dance taking place.

For the floor of the hall was filled with all manner of man and woman. Clothed and unclothed in the dress of many periods. There were Negroes and Indians and Chinese. Some of the men were clearly excited by the naked women (or the scantily clothed) and they would grab or be grabbed by their partners and engage in acts (some of which Malcolm did not know existed—but looked to be intensely pleasurable). And among the men and women there were others. Almost—but not quite—human. They were hard to look at straight on. In fact if Malcolm really stared at them he heard a buzzing in his ears and they would disappear with a kind of pop. But he could see them out of the corners of his eyes. Their noses long and flexible, their dull blue teeth, their tiny horns. There were musicians dancing among the great throng. Players of horns and viols, bone flutes and ebon wood flutes, bagpipes and hautboys. There were rattlers of rattles, drummers of drums, chimers of chimes, and twangers of long stringed instruments Malcolm could not identify. There were those launching whistling rockets, exploding strings of fireworks, and lighting flower-fires of every color.

A beautiful naked Negress danced before Malcolm and plopped a candy in his open mouth. He would have sworn on a stack of Bibles that it was his grandmother's fudge.

The music grew so loud and wild that it got inside him and ran around the inside of his skin and he found himself among them—cavorting and cutting capers as never before. He danced and he sang all kinds of wild, crazy songs. Dirty songs and nursery songs and songs he heard Indians sang. Finally he was

singing wild songs in a language he didn't know, but expected to know at any minute.

Then there were the viands passed from guest to guest. Sweet smoked meat and spicy cakes and unnamable fruits of an unbelievable succulentness.

He drank from crystal goblets and vials of mother of pearl, of the coldest spring water and of the fiercest liquors. Some of these ran down his chest and other dancers licked these away. Once one of the others so cleaned him. He looked down upon her and she brushed his face gently with her wing.

A Presence sat on a throne at one end of the hall. There was a veil of dark fire surrounding him. Whenever there was a pause in the great dance, the dancers would look toward the throne with anticipation.

As Malcolm leaned forward to seize a cake from a silver tray held by a golden-haired midget, a voice rang out:

"MALCOLM Alexander MacKenzie, come FORTH."

It was not volume, but Presence that made the voice so.

The crowd parted for Malcolm as he approached the throne. They looked at him with respect—not with worship or fear, but with respect. He had seen that same look in Hamlet's eyes when Hamlet spoke to him. But he had never seen so much of it as here—and sadly had never realized its name till now.

The dark fire didn't throw off much heat, but it concealed whoever sat behind it.

"I wasn't expecting you, Malcolm A. MacKenzie. I was expecting your son, but no matter, you are here and I will receive you. It's a little loud here. Let's go to below decks."

Instantly they were in a quiet dark room. The dark fire gave off as much light as a dying campfire.

Two great windows formed the back walls of the diamond-shaped room. Malcolm could see towers with rings of lights illuminating a city and casting ripples of light into a long river.

The Presence spoke to him, "Beautiful, aren't they? They open up the night. That is the city of Austin. They put those 'Moonlight Towers' in two years ago. They're powered by the

hydroelectric plant at that dam. Only two cities with electric lights now, Austin and London. But someday all the world will have them. Light to open up the night. I haven't been this excited in millennia."

"You some kind of inventor?"

"I am every kind of inventor, but you're my best invention. You might say I'm the shaper of your consciousness."

Malcolm seemed a little at a loss. The other continued.

"Oh I wish your son had come. I could've shown him the engines of this craft or talked philosophy with him or let him steal my pot of gold and my singing harp. You don't even know that I made a joke."

"My boy wants to know the secret of the airship."

"Electrical power, diesel engines, helium. Aluminum. Rotors. Calculating machines. I've told everyone."

"Everyone? But I thought it was a secret."

"People remember what they want to remember. They would learn more if they studied the people I move to find their way here."

"Don't you just pick up and bring them?"

"The salve does that. The witches' ointment. Broom grease. Really one of my best inventions except that it screws up the memory. Selling it through the Sears and Roebuck catalog was a stroke of genius."

The airship had begun to move away from Austin. The Moonlight Towers seemed to move into one another becoming one light and then a star and then naught.

"Where are you taking me?"

"On the wild ride, Malcolm? I wanted to check on Galveston before dawn."

"I've never seen the ocean. I was born in Georgia, but I've never seen it. My brother sent some shells to my boy."

"Curiosity is strong in him. I can feel that. He's as brave as you are and curious. He's the kind of man who will make the twentieth century."

The involved darkness below was moving rapidly now.

Lakes and ponds threw the stars and moon back at the airship. Malcolm saw the glowing cone of a charcoal-maker's mound burning out of control. He could see the birds—some sort of white bird—that seemed to glow in the moonlight. And then there were strands of cotton, which he realized were clouds. They were above the clouds. Those were clouds down there. And he couldn't even feel it, couldn't even feel them moving.

"Will we really see the ocean?"

The voice was gentle for the first time, "Yes. Remember, remember the ocean."

"Have you been at this inventing for a long time?"

"In Egypt such nights were called Typhonia. By your standards it's been a long time."

"Why?"

"For a bet. To prove myself right."

"Yeah, I know how that is. I once bet Bedford Derleth I could walk twenty-five miles in one day. And I did. My feet were sore for weeks. That pride can be a heavy thing."

The Presence laughed.

Malcolm asked, "This guy you bet, is he keeping track of all the stuff you do?"

"I don't know. I haven't seen Him for awhile."

* * * * * * *

The airship was passing over plains of coarse grass. There were farms and marshes full of moonlight. And then.

The ocean.

It was everything he'd dreamt of. Everything people said. And more and different. He watched the lines of white foam markers of waves and beyond that there was movement without the great lines—just isolate flecks of white. And it went on forever.

The airship turned around over an island. There were fine brick buildings in the moonlight—and tall-masted ships tied up round the island and a bridge as pretty as a picture of the new

Eiffel Tower bringing two ribbons of railroad steel to the island.

"Say, eh, Mister, what did you bet?"

"I bet that people could learn to think for themselves."

The airship had turned landwards.

"That's some bet. I want my son to think for himself, but when he starts to, it scares me."

"Diversity brings more than it takes away. That's why I hate slavery. You lose diversity."

"I'm really glad to see the ocean. Could you show me your face so I know who did all this?"

"No one's asked me that for a while." The Presence stepped through the veil of dark fire. There was never skin so black as pure ebon as this. There were never eyes so full of stars nor leather wings so frightening. But above all, here was the most beautiful face—even with its marks of pride and anger—that Malcolm A. MacKenzie had ever seen. Of course it was one of the foremost of its species.

Now theologically Malcolm wasn't prepared for this instant. He thought what he was seeing was God. He dropped to his knees.

Instantly all beauty changed to anger. The creature seized Malcolm with its taloned hand. It burned into the flesh like a branding iron. It hauled Malcolm to his feet.

"NEVER. NEVER KNEEL. Stand on your own feet!"

The dark fire surrounded the creature again, and Malcolm thought he heard the creature say, "It's part of the bet." But the words were so soft he wasn't sure.

* * * * * * *

Malcolm woke in his kitchen. Dawn light was reddening the windowpanes.

A dream, he thought, it was a dream.

Then he moved and almost passed out from the charred places on his shoulder.

He got dressed which wasn't easy since every movement

brought a whimper from his throat. He threw the rest of the salve on the banked coals of the fireplace where it burned nastily.

Roberta found him drinking coffee cups full of whiskey. He wouldn't let her go for the doctor, but she did ride into town and find Hamlet. Hamlet came back to the ranch. Malcolm wouldn't talk about his experience, but Hamlet had a good idea.

In fact, Malcolm talked less and less as the years went by. He'd just saddle up his horse and ride to a high spot on the ranch and watch the stars, but folks never knew why.

The ranch prospered under Hamlet's management. In fact, it became something of a model of modern ranching techniques. Hamlet married Rosa, and she got her share of the ranch—which was all she ever wanted anyway. Some evil-eyed gossips said that the ranch had begun to prosper because Rosa had taken her spell off it.

As for Emily Jones, the town got the railroad the next year; and Emily rode off with the conductor beyond the boundaries of this tale.

(for John A. Keel)

GRAVY RUN

Nobody loves the bread man when it snows. Each store owner bitches because the bread's late. The dock hates you because they hate everybody when Christmas season comes with sixteen-hour days. Even your girlfriend's miffed because she hasn't seen you in weeks.

The roads want to kill you. The snow merges road and land. The ice pulls at your truck. Your brothers' and friends' trucks fill the ditches and you drive on by—at twenty miles an hour— because you're already eight, twelve, sixteen hours late.

My last drive for Soft-n-Fresh bakery came with the worst storm of the season. December 21. I had to take 63, an old bobtail with no heater and damn near no brakes. I put my print-outs in order, closed my brown garage sale briefcase, and drank my last cup of coffee. I said goodbye to the dockworkers. The fat kid said, "Try to be back before Christmas." And I laughed. Then I opened the door and saw he wasn't joking.

The truck started on the third try and I pulled out of the bay. About a mile down the road I switched on the radio. Nothing but static. Beats Christmas carols I guessed.

My first stop was in Canyon, Texas. Usually they've got a cup of coffee waiting for me. That day it was just sullen looks and complaints. I set up the rest of my route in their parking lot. They'd given me ten extra boxes of SoftyCrust. In addition to everything else I was supposed to peddle extra bread today.

My next ten stops were all little towns. No chance of talking them into buying extra bread. Night fell. I crossed into New

Mexico. Snow fall lightened a little. I could see twenty maybe thirty feet in front of my truck. The plows had been through recently so the going got easier. About midnight—about halfway to Tucumcari—I spotted a hitcher.

Now I don't pick up hitchers. I've got a scar over my left ear from my last encounter with one. So normally I just wave and drive on. But I figured leaving someone out on a night like this was tantamount to murder. I stopped.

The old man climbed in. His hair and beard were white with snow. He grabbed my thermos as I started up. He drank half of it in one glup. Then he started talking, "Glad I found you."

I figured the snow had got to him; I said, "You mean glad I found you."

"No, son, I've got a great business opportunity for you."

I didn't like the sound of that.

He went on, "It's about those ten boxes of SoftyCrust."

For the first time tonight my insides got colder than my outsides. I said, "What do you know about my load?"

"I'm a businessman, son, a businessman."

I looked him over carefully. He wore a plain quilted coat over a dirty red flannel shirt, levis, tore-up boots. He didn't look like the Devil or Merlin or an escapee from a B-movie. But his eyes, well, his eyes gleamed like the snow.

I hate it when someone calls me "son." I said, "Sure, pops, sure. What's the deal?"

"I'm gonna arrange for you to sell the bread at a huge profit."

"It isn't my bread. It's the bakery's."

"You can pay them for it. And still make a huge profit."

"What do you get, my soul or something?"

"Just ten per cent of your take. It'll be enough to capitalize my researches for years."

He talked like a businessman.

"Why did you pick tonight? I got extra bread lotsa times."

"Because of the snow. You know the saying back in Amarillo? 'The only thing between Amarillo and the North Pole is a barbed wire fence' then when it's real cold they say 'Somebody musta

took the fence down'?"

"I've heard it."

"Well, it's truer than they know. Only it's not the North Pole."

I figured I'd picked up a nut. He'd guessed right about the bread. So what? Extra bread on my run is a certainty. I decided to turn him over to the Tucumcari police. They could lock him up safe and warm. So I said, "Sure, pop, you just take care of everything."

To my surprise he went to sleep. He snored. At two in the morning his pocket alarm went off. *Beep!Beep!Beep!* I hate those things. He sat up. He pulled a little silver case from his shirt pocket. I thought he was going to offer me a cigarette. He pressed a button.

The truck skidded off the road straight into an electrical substation. The substation bent away from the truck just before the impact. It pulled back like rubber. A little tunnel formed and sucked the truck into it. Lightning flashed on the tunnel walls. The truck shrank into a string. Everything elongated. I got dizzy—no dizzy's too mild a road. I turned toward the old guy. He was grinning. Then his silver case blew up. He said, "Damn!" then he disappeared. Everything went black.

I came to. The cab was O.K—I guessed the rest of the truck was. It set on a low snow-covered plain. The sun was shining. It was surrounded.

They stood in a rough circle around my truck. Their eyes were orange, their fur white. I'd guess they were eight feet tall. They carried spears.

I opened my briefcase and took out my .45. The first spear smashed through my windshield. The glass cut my cheeks. I fired at the spear thrower. A bad miss, but the noise scared them. They screamed like monkeys in a Tarzan picture. I lay across the seats trying to provide as little target as possible. Spears hit the hood. I fired out the passenger's window wounding one. It went crazy. It grabbed its reddening side and charged the truck. I fired two more times. It fell. Then they were on me. From everywhere.

I came to again. They had tied me to a tree. Night had fallen and two moons rose. One was pink the other yellow and brown like a giraffe. Both circled that world closer than our moon does Earth or perhaps they're much larger.

Near me stood ten breadboxes. The snow creatures danced around a pyre. In the center of the flames lay the one I shot. They howled. They seemed happy. Maybe I'd shot the boss.

I could move my left hand. I reached my jeans' pocket and found a piece of the windshield. I began cutting my bonds. The snow creatures were passing around a bowl full of drink. I cut myself free and ran for my truck. The ground looked level enough to drive on.

Something was in the cab. I put the glass between my knuckles. I pulled my door open. The old guy slammed my briefcase shut. He said, "Sorry about all this" then hit a button on his little box.

The New Mexico highway patrol dug me and my truck out of the ruins of the substation. They said I was drunk—talking incoherently. Soft-n-Fresh paid all my hospital bills then let me go.

I went out to the bakery to pick up my last check. I decided not to tell them anything. What could I say? The fat kid took my stuff to my beat-up old Impala while I was in the front office. He stared at me funny as I drove off.

I could barely pick up my briefcase at home. I set it on the table. I opened it. The snow creatures had paid for the bread. The briefcase was full of gold nuggets. None were smaller than my thumb.

First thing I'm going to do is move someplace warm.

THE MARTIAN SPRING OF DR. WOODARD

Warm. Alive. Humming. It pressed upon her groin. Her outer lips opened and the saucer sent a tiny probe to rest on the gristly button of her clitoris. Sharon came slowly and powerfully. The small saucer settled slightly—abandoning itself to its work. Her arms and legs writhed about seeking a lover to hold. The white-hot energy flowed through her again. She clutched her sheets hard to hold onto this world to keep from dissolving in the pleasure. The saucer lowered its vibration to something bone-shaking and her labia fell out wet around its base hugging the shiny metal with her granular pink folds. Another orgasm intense as the second rushed through.

(It will kill me this time.)

The saucer lessened its pressure preparatory to leaving. A gentler orgasm answered it—almost the response to a lover's kiss. The saucer rose a few inches above Sharon's cunt. She felt her own juices drip in a fine rain on her thighs. It darted off behind her chest of drawers. She lay still for a while, enjoying the electric aftershocks of lovemaking.

(This isn't getting my work done.)

She rose and stripped the orange satin sheets off her bed. They were too damp and would be unpleasant when she returned to bed in three hours. She had given herself over to such hedonisms after the saucer had come to stay. It was good to feel good.

In the shower she resisted her vagina's call for more stimula-

tion. Her limbs were weak enough as it was. She busied herself with thoughts. She had little to think of—little new to think of until the saucer had arrived and changed her life into science fiction. Every year the same classes. English masters to sophomores, English zero—composition—to freshmen. She waited every year for some old fart to die or retire so she could aim for a tenured slot. Her mind had been alive the first year she came here. She'd added two women to the "Masters" list. Shelly and Woolf. And she'd had to fight to do that.

Now her mind was alive again. Mainly she thought about the saucer. Where did it come from? Why is it here? Why me? She began reading a great deal of scientific material. First the pop things: Asimov and Sagan. Now she's on the Scientific American level. All her politics had been the vague institutionalized leftism of the academic. Now she saw how small our planet is, how much it needs to be managed. She wrote a *New York Times* Op Ed piece condemning the destruction of the Amazonian rain forest.

The Tenure Committee thought it was an attempt to gain attention.

She'd begun to read science fiction, too. Doris Lessing, Ursula K. Le Guin, Joanna Russ.

She turned off the water, toweled herself, put on her navy-blue terry cloth robe. She started the cocoa and sat down to the English Zero essays. Five paragraph exposition. Her five-principle hypothesis on the origin of the six-inch saucer.

1. It was constructed by a love-sick engineer in the EE department. Confused by dopplering radio sources during the night of the falling stars, it wandered over to the field I stood in.

2. Unbelievably ancient, the saucer belonged to the culture that existed on the fifth planet (between Mars and Jupiter). It lay fossilized in an asteroid till it was burned free by the asteroid's descent into the earth's atmosphere.

3. Extremely tiny beings inhabit this space ship. They're recharging its battery with my nervous energy. (Charge away.)

4. It's a probe. Whether or not it's functioning as its makers intended is indeterminable.

5. It is a figment of the imagination.

(No.)

She graded the thirty-two essays. She made her bed and lay down. She waited for a moment to see if the saucer would visit her again. Then drifted off to sleep.

* * * * * * *

Earlier in the term—a fortnight after the saucer came to visit her—she'd found the note from Nadine Older.

Nadine was all the things that she had been: pretty, smart, quiet, and the possessor of an elfin sense of humor.

She was still all those things. Wasn't she? Pretty except for an ugly birthmark that wandered down her forehead and across her left eyelid. She knew the engineering students called her "Mikhail Gorbachev." Nadine could've been from her clone tank except Nadine lacked a blemish. It's rare to see a beautiful mind in an English Masters class.

The note was to "Bob." It read, "Dr. Woodard is an O.K. teacher especially if you like spotty warthogs."

Sharon Woodard folded up the note and put it in her purse. It's still there.

* * * * * * *

By midterm the saucer's nightly ministrations had transformed her. She spent long hours in the library. She read everything. She talked. She smiled. She found she could will people to come over and talk to her. Even her classes noticed. She sparked them to life with her quick thinking, her ability to improvise endlessly.

She wrote a few poems for the inevitable small magazine published on campus. Neoneoneon. They weren't good poems— chips off the old Thoreau—but she was writing again.

She was reaching everybody. Was she reaching Nadine?

She assigned Milton's "Lycides" for the Masters class, told the Zeros that she wanted a three-page paper on what they did over break (mainly she wanted them to demonstrate the seventeen uses of the comma) and went to the school pub with Dr. Brandon.

There'd been a brief and boring affair with Brandon the first year she taught here. Brandon's public self was correct politics, parafeminism, and an endless devotion to Beat writing. Brandon's private self was junk food, avoiding the writing of anyone younger than he (47), and a bedroom traditionalist. That means two minutes in the missionary position—then roll over and go to sleep. He also snored.

They split a pepperoni pizza and a bottle of white wine. He told her about the end-of-term bash that some friend of his in the Geology department had every year. A form of teacher-student bonding he called it. These psych profs.

She walked home. She had an intense session with the saucer, mounting it and flying around the inside of her ivy-covered house like a witch on her favorite broomstick. The next morning slightly hung-over she decided on having a bash.

* * * * * * *

The party would be the last Friday before Dead Week. The Masters class should've turned in their last papers by then and the Zeros would have a final counting only fifteen percent of their grade in a week. On Monday she invited her sixty students. On Tuesday she went to the red brick pseudo-Spanish psych building to get some information from Brandon.

"The party's this Friday at 7:30. I have about sixty students— I guess about forty will show up. How much beer do you think I should buy?"

Brandon revealed that the surprising ratio of a half-gallon per student was necessary. (God, they drink like fishes when it's free.) She calculated the number of kegs. She invited Brandon,

who declined, but advised her in the inevitable Brandon manner on the kinds of potato chips, peanuts, and dips she would need to "do it right."

The rest of the week seems to go by quickly. The party replaced the recent extraterrestrial core of her thoughts. Her excitement made saucer sex better, a change she would've thought impossible. The party: how to have things just right, how the students will think of her as a great gal as well as a fine teacher. Maybe the three or four English majors will overcome their shyness and talk with her about the rewards, spiritual and financial, of teaching. (The long and the short of it.) Of course, she mustn't let them monopolize her time. She must mingle with the others, even the engineering students and the athletes—two groups whom she felt had the greatest antagonism to her and her course. Maybe she could reach the engineers with her newly-won knowledge of physics, cosmology, and information science. Tuesday afternoon talking with a History teacher, she learned that students' opinion had labeled her "the most interesting teacher on campus." According to the History teacher, whom Sharon knew very slightly, "the campus connoisseurs prefer Lone Star Draft. Just think of the initials L.S.D." Sharon liked the phrase "campus connoisseurs " linking it with the previous labeling. She thought that the fellow might be having her on about the L.S.D. Nevertheless, she planned to buy two shiny sixteen-gallon kegs Friday afternoon. No use taking chances, the fellow might be right as well as phony.

Thursday night the saucer skimmed over her bush several times before settling down to work. These butterfly passes got her real hot and the instant the saucer settled on her she came. It rocked back and forth as it vibrated. Perhaps it was trying to overwhelm her—drive the party from her mind.

(This time I surely will die.)

It didn't depart after the fourth orgasm as it usually did. On the tenth orgasm Sharon lost consciousness.

* * * * * * *

She was inside the saucer. Whether she had shrunk or it had grown was unknown. It skimmed along over a barren red landscape. They crossed a vast canyon—bigger than anything in Sharon's life. The saucer lit on a table-like rock. Sharon desaucered.

Wait. Watch.

Other saucers, hundreds of them, skimmed over the horizon. They formed a single long line several (apparent) meters above her. First one flashed. Then another. Then both. Then a third. She realized she was seeing binary counting. The flashings became too quick to follow. After they had run through the numbers possible they ran through patterns—powers of 3, 5, and 7. Finally the primes—up to six-figure binary-notation primes.

The saucers reformed into a plane and ran through several simple geometric figures, a visual demonstration of the Pythagorean theorem, and the simpler curves. The saucers regrouped again into the Platonic solids.

Finally one saucer (her saucer?) hovered over her head. She felt herself drawn out through her head. All her thoughts and feelings going into the saucers which arranged themselves into a complex hyperspiral to model her pattern. Although she was completely inside the pattern, she somehow saw the pattern, her body on the red ground far below, and the two moons passing overhead.

Then each saucer communicated to her at each point. They were small living beings not artifacts, born in the fluxions of a nebula light years away. More than this—other than the feeling of reaching—they could not communicate. She couldn't change the morphology of her mind. Her cells didn't float freely in space.

* * * * * * *

She woke exceptionally clearheaded. The saucer was hovering over her head. It ducked quickly behind the chest of drawers.

It was Friday, the day of the party. She didn't need to go in. She'd canceled her classes, but she was dedicated to her office hours even if her students weren't. Everything spoke to her. The cottonwoods around the English building acquired a fantastic ornateness, a life bomb exploding with a fluorescence of new branches and foliage. Each wisp of cotton, the trees' seeds, was a tiny star falling on the arabesques of Bermuda grass. She saw the environment she wanted to save was here, too. With a sense of loneliness she went inside the dark English building.

Images from her own bad poetry loomed around her: the echoes of her steps on the terrazzo floor, the sunlight on the stairs, the solid wall of leaf outside her window.

It was 9:00. She was early. She realized she wanted to remain in her office all day in case any student wanted to ask directions to her house or just came by to talk to her. She had been too shy to talk to her professors as an undergraduate. But she wasn't one of those formidable old men, she couldn't understand why none of the students come to see her. She always mentioned her office hours in class. Far too often, judging by the bored looks and rolled eyes. The first time a decade ago when she'd said them, the students wrote them down with such zeal that she was sure she would be besieged by visitors. None had shown up until after the first test. Then the athletes came in to complain about their failing grades. Their bodies radiated hostility like a heater in a winter bathroom, but she was so glad to have a visitor that she even raised their grades—though not as much as they seemed to think they deserved—and kept them there talking to her long after they'd shown a desire to leave. Shuffle their feet on the floor, prepare to stand, stare at the seeming jungle beyond—tired of the missionary. After that no one came, not even after the other tests.

About 11:00 William Derenberger, the Old English specialist, poked his head in and asked about coffee. Sharon responded enthusiastically and he was gone. W.D. was a homosexual with a 6 Kinsey rating and the only member of the department who hadn't put the make on her.

He returned with two large green mugs full of steaming coffee.

A lacuna of idle chit-chat.

Sharon confided that she was worried that no one had dropped by. W.D. told her that was normal, that they would be there. Then he told his droll stories of his year-end bashes. He used to have them, but all the fuss. He couldn't be bothered anymore.

She started to invite him but two ugly possibilities appeared to her. She might spend all her time talking to him and neglect the students or, worse still, W.D. might try to pick up one of the football team.

She had to leave at 3:00 to get the beer. She had to drive through a part of town unfamiliar to her. She'd lived in this town, in this not-too-large town, for ten years and she hadn't been down all the roads. She needs to work on that.

(Two moons in an alien sky.)

She bought the beer and left a large check as deposit for the kegs. She was home by four, putting a string of Chinese lanterns across the midline of the back yard.

At 7:20, ten minutes before the party was officially slated to begin, the doorbell rang. "Thank God." Two of her best students were there, Mary Jenkins and Suzy Floyd. Both were the perfect American nymph as epiphanized in TV commercials. Sharon ushered them through the house and started them on a game of lawn darts. The doorbell rang again and Sharon ran. A group of Zeros, the foreign language contingent, smiled their best smiles at her. She led them to the back wondering if this was the correct moment for the rehearsed piece of joviality. Who's ready for a beer?

In minutes everybody came. Sharon busied herself by giving everyone his first beer or soda—then letting them help themselves. She had to get another box of Dixie cups from her kitchen. Upon returning she saw Nadine Older at the keg and realized she had come in without speaking to her hostess. The snub wouldn't ruin her party.

The students had arrived in groups of two and three, and for

the most part tended to stay that way. Occasionally the groups would merge for a few minutes of conversation or to exchange members. Sharon circulated from group to group intensely aware of the uneasiness her presence generated.

After everyone—including Sharon—had had two or three beers the latent hostility began to recede and signs of acceptance, signifiers of friendship began to be offered. Sharon put on a Timbuk3 album.

(Now they won't think I'm a spotty warthog.)

Some of the students were inside and she went to check on them. A couple of the English majors were shelf-reading her library.

"Like to look at any of 'em, Tom?" She said with what she hoped was geniality, but could be read any number of ways.

(I ought to be able to control my texts.)

In reply Tom pulled out *The Place of Dead Roads* by William S. Burroughs. Sharon smiled, but she was too shy to discuss Burroughs with him.

She retreated to the back yard to the keg. She decided not to get too looped. She tossed her Dixie cup back. The breeze shifted and Sharon smelled pot. She had no objection to marijuana but having pot at a party given by a faculty member for students was distinctly bad politics. The blue vapors rose from behind the yew bush. She walked quietly. She'd just tell 'em to cool it.

There were three students in the darkness. One was Nadine. Nadine was reciting a poem about the spring melting of the Martian polar caps. Too beautiful. Too good. Nadine in contact with one of the saucer people? Why her?

(Why not?)

Sharon went back and started the second keg. She didn't have to use words. If only she could set up the pattern she could say what she wanted to Nadine. No falsehoods only a set of one-to-one correspondences.

She got to talking with one of the boys. Turned out to be from her hometown of Doublesign, Texas. They talked about the high

schools, the skating rink, the parks, and the politics. A good time was had by all.

Sharon renewed the dips. Some of the people were drifting away. One by one they came by and thanked her for a good time. She spotted Nadine at the keg. Red-eyed Nadine, her sclera betrayed a strong dose of the weed. Sharon felt she was falling into the geology of those eyes. She went over to Nadine.

(Not like this. Why am I doing this?)

"Pretty nice party for a spotty warthog to be giving, isn't it?"

"What?"

"I said, 'Pretty nice party for a spotty warthog to be giving.'"

"Oh I'm sorry Dr. Woodard. I didn't know you'd overhear."

(Overhear? Meaning she said it as well.)

Nadine continued, "It's just a dorm expression. You're the Spotty Warthog, Dr. Winchell is Doughnut-Daddy, Dr. Lsiang Wang is Fu Manchu, Dr. Derenberger is Oscar Wilder. It don't, you know, mean anything. In fact I think you're a pretty good teacher."

Nadine was scared by the drunken teacher staring at her. Sharon sensed the fear, but wanted to prolong the encounter to break the barrier down. She saw that Nadine wasn't ashamed of the note. Maybe she didn't even write the note. Slow beer thinking didn't provide a path here. Sharon said, "Thank you."

Sharon wandered back to the house. Over the next half hour everyone left. Everyone told her it was a good party. It wasn't a lie.

(If I'd approached her differently I could've asked her about Mars.)

Sharon turned off the lanterns and picked up the cups. She locked up. She undressed. It was still important. At least her earlier self had told her she was doing the right thing.

(This is the essence of time travel.)

She lay down. The saucer hovered above her. For the first time she spoke to it. Using those tones one reserves for lovers and friends, she said, "It was a wonderful party."

ABOUT THE AUTHOR

DON WEBB was born in 1960 in Amarillo, Texas. His works range from a St. Martin Press mystery series, to poetry, and fiction and nonfiction books on the occult. He attended Rice University and the University of Texas at Austin. Don is the poster child of literary ADHD. He's written a rock-'n'-roll song for French radio, the I-phone App "Office Ching," and has done game design for FASA and TSR. He's also penned a lot of horror stories. His mom says that Don is her favorite horror writer—after Ramsey Campbell! He's been translated into twelve languages; ten of his poems have been published in Chinese in *Selected Poems of Post-Beat Poets*.

He lives in Austin, Texas with his lovely wife Guiniviere and their cats Big Pig and Sascha. He cries at the sight of bluebonnets in the spring, the ending of the *Whole Wide World*, and losses of the Longhorn football team.